Fanita Moon Pendleton

I0538521

Fist Full Of Tears

The Sequel

This is a work of fiction. All of the characters, organizations, and events portrayed in this novel are either products of the author's imagination or are used fictitiously. Any resemblance to actual persons, living or dead is purely coincidental.

Fist Full Of Tears: The Sequel

Acknowledgments

My son is the light of my life. Helping him grow into a young man has been the single most important thing I have ever done. I hope him witnessing me fulfill my dreams encourages him to shoot for his. I love you **Brione Lamont Pendleton**.

Family Shout Out's to my Oakland California Family, Norfolk Virginia Family, Oklahoma Family, Texas Family, New York Family, and Hopkinsville, Kentucky Family.

Special Shout Out to **Mig** for holding **Urban Moon Productions** down with his debut series, **Dirty Red: A Killa's Love Story**….. I love you man. Check out his work on Nook and Kindle.

www.Urbanmoonproductions.com

Follow me on twitter **@Moon081471**

Instagram: Fanita Moon Pendleton

Connect with me on Facebook **Fanita Moon Pendleton**

Website **www.urbanmoonbooksandmore.com**

Email-urbanmoonbooksandmore@gmail.com

Join my Readers Group on Facebook... Fanita Moon Pendleton's Readers

Please be sure to leave your review.

Fanita Moon Pendleton

Shout Out to **Monica Coleman and Wanda Lee and Jamilah** for lending their names to characters in this series: These characters are in no way meant to depict them personally.

Reviews are important to authors they give you a voice, but they are also important to potential readers who want to know from someone who has read the book how they liked it. I appreciate your support............

Fist Full Of Tears: The Sequel

Previously In Book I

Redemption

He noticed Deuce slip away from the crowd as attention was placed on lil Young choking the shit out of Wanda Lee. He smiled because lil Young handled her ass exactly like he was supposed to; walking up on him with that bullshit. He even understood the Young Gunz pulling their guns on lil Young. They were trained to protect each other and for all intents and purposes, lil Young wasn't one of them; so he could get it.

Right now he had to trust Kenyatta would handle that situation because he had to stop Deuce from getting ghost. There was a secret exit to this building not many people knew about, but he did. Moving swiftly he made it there just before Deuce turned the corner and when he did he was met by a strong crack to his jaw and a crack to his head from a gold platted Glock. Deuce dropped to the ground like a large sack of potatoes.

With a satisfied grin on his face all he could say was "Still a bitch ass nigga. You could never take a punch. You always folded up just like a little bitch."

Before Deuce could attempt to recover and retaliate for the assault he was placed in a choke hold from the back and the gun was placed to his head.

"Walk nigga, before I end you right here."

A hard shove in the direction he just left caused Deuce to move forward. The look on Deuce's face was priceless; he looked like he swallowed something sour, but was trying to place the familiar sounding voice. Right before they entered the room they heard a gun fire and lil Young's vow to find Deuce.

There was so much commotion in the room they entered unnoticed for a second, but Deuce's entrance didn't go unnoticed for long. Lil Chop was the first to notice.

"There his bitch ass go right there."

The whole team turned in the direction Lil Chop was pointing and sure enough there was Deuce looking dazed with a gun to his head and a strong arm choking him from behind. Every weapon in the room was pointed at Deuce. It was like an FBI standoff, only everyone in the room was a criminal. Kenyatta was the first to speak up.

"Well Pops, looks like somebody done whopped King Kong ass."

There was a deep sound of sarcasm and resentment in Kenyatta's voice along with some snickers around the room. Kenyatta looked at lil Young who was two seconds from busting his gun and slowly shook his head no. He refused to let lil Young kill him before he got some answers first. He wanted to know why he allowed him to live a lie for all these years. He wanted to know why he just didn't divorce his mother rather than victimizing her for all these years. Shaking his head Kenyatta was about to get his answers when lil Young yelled out, "And who the fuck is you with the gun. Show yourself before I light your ass up too. Who the fuck are you?"

The eyes of every member of the Young Gunz switched from Deuce to the person emerging from behind him. As he fully revealed himself every mouth in the room dropped to the ground. Some people even had to clear their eyes. He hadn't changed much in ten years; maybe a little more muscle, but other than that it was as if time stood still. Wanda Lee was the first to say something as she yelled out with tears forming in her eyes.

"Is that you Young?"

No one believed what they were seeing. Fist just stood there too shocked to say anything. He couldn't believe what his eyes were trying to tell his brain was true.

Fist Full Of Tears: The Sequel

It was as if the last ten years rushed back and hit him full force; he felt one of his knees buckle, but he refused to go down. He studies his facial features which were almost a duplicate of his own as he shook his head back and forth in disbelief.

It was at this time Blood and Holiday both entered the room with their weapons drawn. They had followed Deuce from the room and witnessed his take down. They were both having a hard time as well, reconciling the fact Young was standing in the room. Blood was staring at him as if his mind's eye were a magnifying glass. Both men stared at each other for what seemed like hours until Blood spoke out.

"Louis, is that fucking you man?"

Young smiled at him because only he would call him Louis. With conviction, pain and death in his eyes he shook his head.

"It's me Junior, or should I call you Blood?"

FIST FULL OF TEARS

The Sequel

FANITA MOON PENDLETON

Fist Full Of Tears: The Sequel

Anyone Can Get It

The ringing in his ears was causing a piercing headache. Although he refused to give in to the buckling of his knees, he could feel himself getting physically sick. There was no way his eyes could be seeing what his brain was telling him was right in his face. Fist considered himself a fairly smart man; a man of integrity and strength, but the feelings he was experiencing right now threatened to jeopardize his sanity. He just stood there too shocked to say anything. It was as if the last ten years rushed back and hit him full force; the screaming of his mother, the devil in his room, the bullet to his head. It was all more than he could take at this very moment. He studied the facial features of the man before him which were almost a duplicate of his own and shook his head back and forth in disbelief. The sound of gun shots broke the trance everyone was in. The killers in the room ducked for cover as smoke filled the open space. Young dropped to his knees and Deuce attempted once again, to flea like the bitch he was. Yatta stopped him in his tracks; the anger and contempt dripped from his voice.

> "Move one more muscle and I will lay you the fuck down."

Wanda Lee and Josey ran over to Young who had been hit twice in the chest. The smoke was still rising from the bullets. Lil' Young stood there with his gun still pointed in the direction of his father; there was a look of confusion and frustration deep in his eyes. No one in the room knew what to do, because everyone was fucked up. Lil' Chop took over watching Deuce and Kenyatta checked on his father as he gave a puzzled look towards Lil' Young.

Fanita Moon Pendleton

The tension was thick and Lil' Young was unapologetic, still holding his chopper in the direction of his father as he said in a tone that dripped with venom

> "This nigga alive. This nigga right here in the flesh after I been through hell for ten years."

Young, breathing hard and holding his chest, was staring into the eyes of his son and felt every bit of the emotions he was going through. He understood his son's pain and wanted to reach out to him. But Young also saw that famous fire in his son's eyes, because it was the same fire he had deep inside. One thing Young knew for sure was if Lil' Young wanted him dead, he would be dead. Shooting him in his chest was out of frustration. He decided it was better to let him collect his thoughts before they both ended up killing each other. Young looked towards his first born, Kenyatta, and taking a deep breath he said,

> "I'm ok son, I'm wearing my vest. Go to your brother; he is hurting and he needs you."

As Young slowly made his way to his feet, he made eye contact with Lil' Young; the questions were hanging in a thick smoke of uncertainty. Young gave his son a strong head nod. He looked towards Blood and Holiday and slowly waved them closer. Everyone was so engrossed in the drama unfolding no one, not even Lil' Chop, noticed Deuce slip away.

Fist Full Of Tears: The Sequel

Monica's Dream

Days passed and Monica still hadn't heard from Young, Fist, or Kenyatta. Being the one in control was something she had begun to relish, but right now control was something she did not have. Resting in luxury, one would think she had the world by the balls, but instead she felt useless and used. It reminded her of the woman she used to be before Young came into her life; it both scared her and pissed her off. Pulling the silk pillow over her face, she screamed at the top of her lungs out of pure frustration as she remembered that lost little girl.

He's ALIVE! Monica, an assistant medical examiner trainee, jumped back from the autopsy table. For a quick minute she didn't know what to do, but her instincts kicked in and she rushed to his side. Just hours earlier, the man was delivered to the medical examiner's office along with a female subject. Monica's job as a trainee was to undress them, and wipe them down to prepare them for examination the next day by the Chief Medical Examiner. The female subject's preparation had already been completed and she was placed in the morgue for refrigeration to delay decomposition. When Monica removed the cover from over the male subject, she laid her eyes on the most beautiful specimen she had ever seen up close and personal. She began thinking, my Lord, who would damage such perfection. Shaking her head, she began to remove his clothes paying close attention to the chiseled abs, muscular chest, and flat stomach. Monica had to stop for a second because she could feel herself getting hot. Fanning herself she knew this had to be a new low, thinking out loud she said, who gets turned on by a dead man?

Fanita Moon Pendleton

Smiling despite herself she answered her own question; well let's see... that would be the nineteen-year-old virgin, that's who. Trying not to laugh too hard at herself, she continued with the task at hand. When she removed his pants and saw he wasn't wearing any underwear, but he was carrying the largest muscled member she had ever laid eyes on, she couldn't control her intake of breath. Monica had seen many dead men's bodies before, but what she was witnessing now was spectacular. The thickness of his dick made her eyes bulge and she couldn't understand why the inside of her mouth was sweating. She felt compelled to reach out and touch it. She looked around the empty room as if someone would see her, almost feeling guilty. She just had to know if it felt as good as it looked; besides, she was supposed to be washing him down anyway. Placing two hands around the thickness, she chuckled as she said to herself I wonder how much it weighs. As she stroked his dick up and down like she had seen on the many movies she watched alone in her apartment, it began to grow thick and strong. She could hear an unescapable moan coming from a man that was supposed to be dead. Monica jumped back, initially thinking someone was playing a trick on her. She looked around and mouthed to no one in particular this is the worst joke ever.

The music in the room was still playing loudly. Monica was breathing hard as she held on to the table to catch her breath. She didn't believe in ghosts or anything like that; she was a more practical person than that. The moaning coming from the table threatened her understanding. Moving slowly towards the table with her mind racing and her heart beating loud enough to be heard over the music, she noticed a forced flickering of his eyelids and she mouthed, He's alive.

Fist Full Of Tears: The Sequel

Monica went straight back into her role as a trainee. She checked his vital signs and immediately knew a medical doctor is what he needed. He had two bullet holes as far as she could see. He'd lost a lot of blood and most likely slipped into a comma, causing everyone to think he was dead. Rubbing a sponge over his wounds, something stirred in her. She was sweating more than she normally did, a sure sign she was in distress. The nervousness in her didn't stop her from coming to the only conclusion that she could.

Monica was going to get him some help without letting the world know he was alive. This went against everything her father taught her, but she was tired of playing it safe all her life. It was obvious to her someone wanted this man dead. Pacing back and forth she began speaking out loud thinking, 'they killed this man's entire family. This is the most inhumane thing I have ever seen. She pulled her cell phone out of her smock and called the only person she knew who would help her without saying she was crazy; her best friend, Velnita. The ringing of the phone was causing wrinkle lines to form on Monica's face. She needed Velnita, not only because she was a surgical nurse, but she also came up with the best ideas and right now, that is exactly what Monica needed. Just when she was about to give up and figure things out on her own, there was an answer.

"Hello." Monica almost didn't recognize the voice so she said "Nita, is that you?"

Fanita Moon Pendleton

The coughing that came through the phone muffled the answer to the question, but hearing Mo-mo coming from the person on the other end let her know it was indeed her girl, because she was the only one who called her Mo-mo. There was an immediate sense of relief that rushed over Monica as she gave the short and dirty version of what was going on. And just like she thought, Velnita said,

> *"I'm on my way Mo-mo."*

Velnita removed three bullets from the man who Monica now knew was Louis Young, Sr. He lost a lot of blood and was in and out of consciousness, but he wasn't dead. Velnita came up with a plan to take one of the fresh unclaimed Jon Doe bodies from the morgue and make that paperwork disappear. That Jon Doe would now become the male subject awaiting autopsy. It was real easy to do if you have an inside person, which is where Monica came in. It took another week for him to regain consciousness. Monica was redressing his bandages when he reached up and touched her hair. He looked dazed but he was smiling as he asked,

> *"Where am I sweetness?"*

Monica was sure she had turned a different shade of pink. She was not used to being talked to by men, especially not ones like him. She didn't care that he was heavily medicated, she turned from him blushing as she said,

> *"My name is Monica and I am going to help you get better."*

Fist Full Of Tears: The Sequel

Young tried to nod his head but it appeared to be too heavy for him to hold up, but he was able to say,

"I saw you in my dream."

Removing the pillow from her head, she sat up quickly in the bed. Reliving how she met Young was bitter sweet. She was so in love with him she could feel it in her soul. He taught her how to value her beauty; he showed her what it was to be a woman. She had never known confidence as a woman until Young took her under his wing, so when he said he wanted her to do something for him, it was no question; it was a done deal. But now things were different. Ten years after the fact she could tell he didn't have any use for her anymore. Young didn't love her the way she loved him. Although he never promised her a future with him, she felt like he owed her his life. And if he wouldn't give it to her, she would take it.

Fanita Moon Pendleton

Meisha's Dilemma

Meisha was still hiding away in the Hilton Hotel. She didn't call it hiding out; she actually felt like she was making plans. She was feeling a little under the weather but she knew she had to make some moves. Fixing herself a cup of coffee, she sat at the breakfast bar and let her mind wander over the mess she made, thinking *I have to take responsibility for my part in this mess. But if Deuce killed Young, fuck my part in it; he has got to get it.* The ringing of her cell phone caused her to jump, slightly spilling her coffee on the counter. She wanted to ignore the cell phone but Kelis' song, "I Hate You So Much Right Now" she chose as his ringtone, made her change her mind. She got up and snatched the phone open; sure enough it said "Ex-Husband". Trying to hold her anger at bay, she answered with a neutral tone.

"Hello."

There was a lot of shifting around in the background before anyone responded, but once he did, Meisha wished the phone call never happened as he screamed,

> "Bitch, where the fuck have you been? I've been by that house five times over the last couple of days and you ain't been there."

He was yelling so loud into the phone she took it away from her ear and let him rant. There was no need to interrupt him, because that would just make him madder. When there was a pause in his theatrics, Meisha said in a calm tone,

Fist Full Of Tears: The Sequel

"I checked myself into the hospital since you tried to kill me the last time I saw you."

There was a growl that came through the line almost sounding like a vicious dog was about to attack. Deuce said with as much heartless venom as he could,

"Bitch I should have killed your no good, hoe ass. But you ain't dead, yet. Get yo' ass back to the fucking house right now."

Before she could reply, he hung up the phone in her ear. For what seemed longer than it was, she stood there with the phone in her hand. Her anger was threatening to boil over. Thinking out loud, she stared across the room. *I am so tired of this nigga it ain't even funny. I should just call my son and tell him where to find his bitch ass, but I ain't gonna do that. I'm gonna take care of Deuce myself. If he wants me to come home, then he better be ready for the bitch that's about to walk through the door.*

Fanita Moon Pendleton

Deuce -They ain't bout this life

After hanging up on Meisha's dumb ass, Deuce just shook his head. His plan was to use her to pull Kenyatta and Young out in the opening. He knew Kenyatta had love for her and wouldn't willingly let her be killed. Deuce planned on playing on this weakness. He was kind of fucked up about Young and Lil' Young being alive though. Pacing around the room with the phone still gripped tight in his hand, he began talking loudly. *I can't believe these motherfuckers are still living, but I'm definitely going to do something about that shit. They think Deuce is a play toy, but I'm about to put them all up on game.* Downing a shot of crown, Deuce laughed at the whole situation saying, *these niggas think they can fuck with me; really? That shit is hilarious. They're so into their damn feelings they let a 'G' nigga like me slip away. Don't they know I am about to fuck their world up AGAIN! These bitch niggas don't even understand the Deuce is WILD!.* There was a knock at the door that interrupted his rant. Grabbing his glock, he slowly made his way to the door at an angel; he refused to be caught slipping again. He was chilling at his down low spot on Jib Court in the Fox Hill section of Hampton. The only person who knew he was there was his cousin, so anybody else was getting a free trip to the morgue. The night sky wasn't giving off light, but the street light near the corner slightly illuminated his block enough to make identification possible. Deuce checked the street with a sniper's vision while his visitor waited patiently at the door. He knew the routine. Satisfied, he swung the door open with a slight grin on his face saying,

Fist Full Of Tears: The Sequel

"'Bout damn time you got here nigga. These fools have lost their damn mind down this bitch."

He slapped hands with Stacks, his cousin from the West Coast. Stacks was in town with a group of hittas ready to help his favorite cousin bring order back in TNT. Jericho "Stacks" Longfellow was standing at the door looking like a Tyrese replica, but taller with dreads hanging down his back. He was smiling at his cousin showing nothing but his Colgate best. It has been eight years since his release from San Quentin Penitentiary. He did ten years for the first-degree murder of his wife, Jaycee. He was initially given life without the possibility of parole, but ten years into his sentence, a scandal was discovered in the Oakland California Crime Lab. The lab was accused of mishandling DNA samples and providing false testimony in court to cover it up. If it wasn't for his cousin hiring the best attorneys in California, straight sharks, he wouldn't be there today chopping it up with him. So there was nothing Deuce couldn't get him to do. He gave his cousin a big hug saying

"Man I had to get everything straight, but you know I was on the first thing smoking to the East. These niggas ain't ready for this West Side connection."

Closing the door they made their way to the living room where Deuce went to fix them both a drink. Stacks was checking his surroundings out. The room was spacious with white carpet. He almost didn't want to walk on it, but Deuce waved him in. Cocaine white couches with large, fluffy pillows were the centerpiece of the room. Two oversized paintings hung over the white marble fireplace.

Fanita Moon Pendleton

One was of a beautiful naked black woman sitting on a black throne and the other of a beautiful naked black woman sitting on a white throne. Stacks was still staring at the paintings when Deuce returned with their drinks. Stacks took his drink and pointed to the picture saying,

> "Cuzzo, so what's up with these? This ain't even yo' style."

Deuce burst out laughing cause he knew he fucked Stacks up with the paintings, but he would understand the symbolism. He said walking closer to the fireplace looking up at the paintings,

> "You know what cuz, in a way it is me. See part of me still wants a woman to be the Queen in my life, shit that's what I wanted for Meisha's ass. But then the other part of me just wants a woman to be butt naked and silent. I don't trust any of their asses anymore, and that's on everything."

Shaking his head, he turned to his older cousin talking louder then he meant to.

> "Meisha done fucked shit up for any woman to be anything more to me than something to hang on my trophy case. Fuck love and everything that even look like it, feel me."

Stacks knew this was a sensitive area for his cousin, but he could relate. Hell, he did kill his wife. Jaycee thought she was slick when she was creeping with Marquez from the Diablo Set; she thought she was protected. But Stacks didn't get his nickname lightly.

Fist Full Of Tears: The Sequel

He'd been stacking bodies since he was a teenager and had gotten real good at it by being patient. Standing in the sea of white watching his cousin, he lost focus thinking about that time in his life.

He watched them for weeks while he planned just how he would make Marquez disappear and Jaycee pay for her disloyalty. On the night he killed them both, he was sitting back in his 'coupe thinking about how Jaycee's death would affect Harlem; she was only four and she was the spitting image of her mother. He shook off the feelings. There was no way he could allow her to live after she showed she couldn't be trusted; it was unforgiveable. He couldn't do it, even for Harlem. There was only one light on in the house and it was illuminating from one of the upstairs bedrooms. Well actually Stacks knew exactly which room since he had already been inside of the house. Entering the house, he quietly moved the couch in the living room to the side, and placed plastic wrap on the floor. With that accomplished, he stealthily made his way up the stairs towards the loud moans coming from the bedroom. With each step his heart closed more, shutting out the unconditional love he once had for his wife. Standing in the doorway, he could see Marquez pounding into Jaycee from the back. Her round firm ass was hiked in the air like she was the center on a Super Bowl bound football team. Her face was smashed into a satin pillow and she was clutching the side of the bed for dear life. The sounds of skin smacking skin and the headboard slamming into the wall, only made Stacks' trigger finger itch more as he thought, this is a grimy bitch and it's a must she gets this work. Moving with the precision of the martial artist he was, Stacks put a choke hold around Marquez that threatened to snap his neck in two.

Fanita Moon Pendleton

Jaycee jumped up from the bed but before she could get the scream from her vocal cords, her eyes darted between the gun that was pointed at her and her husband's lethal eyes. Piss ran down her legs because she knew her deadly game had come to an end. Stacks looked at her with the grin of the grim reaper and said,

> *"That was your last fuck; I hope it was real good."*

Motioning with the gun for her to move towards the door, he dragged a struggling Marquez by his neck all the way to the living room. Jaycee stepped onto the plastic wrap with heavy feet. She knew what time it was. Stacks released Marquez and pushed him down onto the plastic. Through coughs, he didn't have sense enough not to talk shit saying,

> *"Do you know who the fuck I am esa? I'm a Diablo; you can't kill me esa!"*

Stacks chuckled a little bit as he watched the disgrace in front of him. Marquez had that Spanish black mixture going on; sort of looked like Shamar Moore with a little more Spanish tint to him. But right now he was sounding like a straight bitch to Stacks. Swinging the glock, he knocked Marquez across his head saying,

> *"I know exactly who the fuck you are. You are the dead man that's been fucking my wife. Well I hope the pussy was worth it 'cause it's your last taste of that gushy stuff."*

Fist Full Of Tears: The Sequel

The sound from the glock took the atmosphere in the room by surprise. The silencer on his glock muffled the sound, but the two jacketed hollow point bullets that passed through Marquez's skull caused a loud gasp to escape from Jaycee, as she watched the head of her lover explode and his body fall limp onto the plastic.

> *"Get your ass over here, wrap ya man up and shut the fuck up with that noise. You should have known it would come to this. Who in the fuck do you think you're playing with?"*

Stacks released this venom to Jaycee and she scrambled to do as he said, hoping he would spare her life. She did love him, and she definitely loved Harlem. But lately she was feeling the need to explore and try new things. She just didn't know how to tell Stacks she wanted to move on from the marriage without him exploding and blowing things out of proportion, like now. Stacks watched as Jaycee did a piss poor job at wrapping up the body thinking, she could never be a real ride or die bitch. Hell a real ride or die bitch would have had that shit wrapped up tight like virgin pussy. Shaking his head, he motioned for her to come closer as he said,

> *"The only thing you ever did for me was give me Harlem and for that I will always be grateful.*
> *But you have proven yourself to be a vindictive bitch and for that you got to go."*

Before Jaycee could even open her mouth, the shot ended her life. Her body fell on the plastic with a loud thump. Stacks stared at her as she took her last breath and death invaded her eyes.

Fanita Moon Pendleton

He couldn't determine how he was feeling, but what he did know was he did what he had to do. He thought to himself, if she would cross me for some dick, she would cross me for some paper.

Deuce calling his name brought him back from his inner most thoughts. Still holding his glass of Crown, he tried to play it off like he had been listening the entire time saying,

> "Yeah cuz, I know exactly how you feel, believe me."

The cousins spent the next couple of hours making plans to burn the city down and rebuild an empire from its ashes.

Fist Full Of Tears: The Sequel

Round Table

A week after the warehouse shooting, Holiday was attempting to broker a meeting between Fist, Kenyatta and Young. He knew a consensus had to be worked out, especially since Deuce was out there. They all knew the other shoe was about to drop very soon. If Deuce would go as far as to attempt a massacre on an entire family over what he feels is the ultimate betrayal, then only imagine how much more dangerous he is now. The tension in the room was thick enough to slice with a machete. Young was at the head of the table dressed in Armani slacks and a crisp white button down. He looked every bit the part of the distinguished business man and nothing like the dangerous killer he was. Kenyatta sat next to his father wearing a pair of black True Religion sweatpants and a starched, stiff, white wife beater. There was a look of contempt on his face. He understood how Lil' Young could be pissed at Young. He did get his mother killed on some bullshit. But that wasn't what had Yatta all fucked up. What had him fucked up was that Lil Young and Fist were the same people. Kenyatta remembered walking in on Monica masturbating to a nigga named Fist. Staring a hole through his brother, he was now wondering if this lil' nigga was fucking his mother and his girl.

Fist was sitting on the other side of the table, relaxed in his Gucci shorts and Timbs. He wasn't feeling the looks coming from the other side of the table but he just shrugged his shoulders and said *fuck em*. Fist felt like he had every right to feel like he did and whoever didn't like it could suck his dick. He had no plans to have a family reunion, and it was only on the strength of Holiday and Blood he even showed up today.

Fanita Moon Pendleton

When Blood came to him yesterday, he told Fist how far back he actually went with Young. Blood told Fist about the list they wrote of the five things they wanted to be when they grew up and the one thing that was on both of their lists was hit man. Blood shared with Fist that when Holiday saw him in the hospital, he knew exactly whose son he was and the bond his older brother had with Young. Fist took all the information in Blood was sharing with him. He didn't understand why they kept this a secret from him. Fist felt like it probably would have helped him get over some of his rough days to know he was with people who actually knew his father. He decided not to make a big deal out of it since both Blood and Holiday have always done right by him. There was only one thing he needed to know. Blood sat at the kitchen table nursing a Jack and coke with the same serious look he always wore. Fist was drinking a bottled water and taking in all of the information that had just been placed in his lap, when he said,

> "Blood, you've always looked out for me. You treated me like your son and I could never repay you for that. I ain't even gonna question why you just now telling me this shit. I just want to know if you knew he was alive, that's all."

Placing his glass down on the table, Blood's head was moving from left to right as he said,

> "When I saw him I couldn't fucking believe it. I probably mourned him just as much as you did. Being able to raise you into the man I know he would be proud of was partly me being loyal to your father. I didn't know, but I damn sure am happy he is."

Fist Full Of Tears: The Sequel

Fist pushed away from the table quickly with a fury in his eyes; Bloods voice tried to break through.

> "I always liked Jamilah and I am sorry for your loss; nothing can replace a mother. Did he fuck up? Yes. But he is here now, and if you throw that away you are sentencing yourself back into the hell you have been in for ten years. If nothing else, I know your mother wouldn't want that. Holiday has set up a meeting with Young for tomorrow and I expect to see you there." With that said Blood pushed up from the table and left the room without another word, leaving Fist with his thoughts.

So here he was staring right through his father. This was the man who he looked up to all his life; the man he mourned so deeply at times it threatened his sanity. Yet, this was the same man that put his entire family in jeopardy over some pussy. Fist shook his head as he looked deep into the eyes of the man who brought him into the world. He just couldn't understand how he could move so reckless.

Young understood why his son was so pissed at him. As he sat at the table and made eye contact with Lil' Young, the hurt was evident. He beat himself up over it for the last ten years. He lost his memory for a while from his injuries, but once he regained everything it was even harder on him. At the time he believed Lil' Young to be dead as well. But now was the time for them to find a way to get through the hurt and become a team. Young was not built for bullshit and only the man up above knows how much he loves his sons; but he was losing patience with Lil' Young.

He respected his son's gangsta and for the sake of his mother's memory, he was gonna try one more time. He stood up from the round table and looked at his son

> "All of this shit that went down, I take full responsibility for my role in it. I put you and your momma in harm's way and that was never my intention. I know that probably doesn't help you, but you needed to hear it from me."

Fist's temperature was rising the entire time Young was talking. One thing was for sure and that was none of the bullshit was bringing his mother back. He banged both hands on the table. The frustrations and emotions were threatening to make him fuck something up as he said,

> "I wanna dead this nigga for what he did to my mother, that's real, but as for the rest of this shit - y'all can have it."

Pointing his finger at Young he continued.

> "You should have stayed dead because yo' ass is dead to me."

He looked at his brother and shook his head and said,

> "This nigga ain't even claim you, but you know what... do you homie, I'm out."

Fist got up from his seat so fast the seat went flying to the back of the room. Yatta started to get up too, but Young raised his hand saying,

Fist Full Of Tears: The Sequel

"Let him go. He is feasting off a lot of pain and hurt, and I can dig it." Raising his voice a little he caught Fist's attention before he made it all the way to the door saying, "But youngin let me put this in ya ear."

Fist stopped in his tracks, though part of him wanted to keep going; but the lost son deep down inside of him wanted to hear what his daddy had to say.

"I spent the last two years of my recovery looking for you, after I went to your mother's grave and I could never find a grave for you. Once I found you, I had to get to the bottom of what happened before I came back just so I wouldn't put you in that type of danger again. I love both of my sons. Kenyatta was safer not knowing about me. I made sure I was present in his life every day and you never knew a day I wasn't a daddy to you. So believe me when I say this from my heart to both of you I'm sorry for how shit got fucked up because I couldn't keep my dick in my pants."

He took a breath and looked between both of his sons who were paying close attention as he continued.

"But also believe this... I'm not gonna spend another day on what happened in the past other than to skin this nigga Deuce alive. You either fuck with me or you don't. If you don't, I'll understand. If you do, I'll understand, but the disrespect will stop today. Ride or die with that, but believe it." The firmness of his threat was not missed by anybody in the room.

Fist was looking between Young and Yatta with a burning desire to put something hot in both of their asses, but he knew it wouldn't be an easy lick. He left the room without another word. Young watched his namesake leave and part of him ached. He wanted an open arm reunion with his boys, but fuck it, wasn't shit he could do about it but let Fist rest on it. Turning towards Kenyatta he said,

"Let's get to work."

Fist Full Of Tears: The Sequel

Blood Relative

A week later Blood sat in Club Drizzle nursing a drink, thinking about the last time he saw Young; it was at his wedding to Jamilah. Both men let life and distance get in the way. When Blood heard the entire family was murdered, it hurt him to his heart. Young was around through all of the abuse Blood and Holiday suffered at the hands of their father. There were many times when Blood ran away from home only to end up at Young's house hiding. He could remember his father banging on Young's door looking for him and Young acting like he didn't know where Blood was. The bond between the two was formed over those hard times. They would spend countless hours together as teenagers, planning out their lives. They wrote a list of the five things they wanted to be when they grew up and the one thing that was on both of their list was hit man. Sitting in a back booth in the back of the club, Blood was now waiting for his friend to show up. Everything was fucked up and he felt stuck in the middle. He wanted to see Lil' Young and his dad work through their problems, but he also knew neither would kiss the other's ass to make it happen. He wanted to be the mediator between the two as he believed he was the only one thinking rationally, but he promised Holiday he wouldn't push the issue too far. As he sipped his Hennessey and watched people go about their day, Blood wondered how he would maintain a meaningful relationship with the man he looks at like a brother and the man he thinks of as a son.

Fanita Moon Pendleton

The music played low. The song was one Young had been hearing playing heavy on the radio. He still couldn't quite place the name of it. He bopped his head to the beat anyway, as he made his way over to where Blood was seated sipping out of a small glass. Young looked around Drizzle; it hadn't changed much since the last time he was there ten years earlier. He could still recall that night like it was yesterday. It was the night before his world changed and the last time he kicked it with Ozone.

Damn this shit is strong, what the fuck she mix this with?" Ozone was laughing so hard at Young as he scrunched his face up from the strong taste of the Hennessey, which was apparently missing the Coke he was used to. Young was a good looking man by any ones standards, standing 6'2 with strong broad shoulders. He kept his fade tight and never stepped out of his house other than razor sharp. Women threw pussy at him all day. His boys joked that he needed to walk around with a catcher's mitt like he was a major league baseball player, the way women acted around him. Young brushed that shit off. He was a married man and dedicated to his family, and his boys could appreciate that.

Young was just a cool ass dude who looked out for his boys, but if the wrong person caught him at the wrong time, he would destroy their world and anybody that looked like them. His gangsta was rarely tested, but when it was, his Young Gunz nipped that shit in the bud quick. Young trained the Young Gunz to stay ready so they never had to get ready. The team was tight; they trained together and played together. Each member of the Young Gunz was like family, and everybody ate in this family.

Fist Full Of Tears: The Sequel

Getting his laughter under control while Young beat his chest from the strong drink, Ozone said,

> *"Aww man, stop being a bitch and take that shit to the head."*

The laughter between the good friends was common place and welcomed. They usually came to Club Drizzle twice a month to catch up and just talk shit to each other. They shared their upcoming vacation plans; Young planned on taking Lil' Young to Disney World and spend some quality time with his family, saying

> *"Lil' Young was psyched about this upcoming trip, and Lord knows Jamilah was ready for a break from VA. I love that woman man and I am going to make sure she has the time of her life."*

Ozone always admired how Young made a commitment to one woman and was being the type of father none of them had.

> *"Man I don't know what Jamilah sexy ass sees in you, but nobody can convince her she can do better."*

Both men burst out laughing. This was an old joke between the two because they met Jamilah at the same time, but Ozone was too busy chasing the big booty chick that she was hanging with to notice the rare beauty right in his face.

Fanita Moon Pendleton

Young took one look at the tastefully dressed, curvy girl with the bright smile and fell hard; that was eight years ago. Now she was his wife and they had a seven year old son. Young was coughing out a laugh.

> *"Whatever happened to the big booty chick that Ja' was with when we first met her? Your ass was sprung on that ass for a minute."*

Ozone was shaking out his laugh as he said,

> *"Man that big booty hoe still be chasing this dick, and that's fine, but the bitch chasing every other dick on the South Side; shit, probably the North, too."*

Pulling himself together, Ozone gave Young a serious look.

> *"Real talk bro, I think you got the last good one with Jamilah and she got a real nigga. All of us not gonna find our Jamilah, but Imma keep fucking these hoes as I look."*

They both fell out laughing again as the waitress came back to their table.

> *"You boys sure are having a good time; can I get y'all something else to drink?"*

Ozone was quick to answer as he gave the pretty waitress the once over.

Fist Full Of Tears: The Sequel

"Yeah pretty lady, bring this nigga right here another one of those strong ass Hennessey mixes."

Young was shaking his head hard from left to right and the waitress had a look like she didn't know what to do, because Ozone was laughing and shaking his head up and down. To save her from her confusion Young said,

"Check it sweetheart... tell the lady at the bar I will take another Hennessey and COKE, not Hennessey and Hennessey."

The waitress gave a slight chuckle to herself as she stared into the sexiest eyes she had ever seen.

"Damn this nigga can get it; all he got to do is say the fucking word," she thought to herself.

Shaking herself from her lustful thoughts, she finished writing down the order making sure to make a special note, because she knew her girl Shaun was all about getting her customers fucked up and she told them as much.

"Yeah, Shaun will make sure to give you your money's worth, but I will tell her."

The waitress turned to walk away deciding she would give an extra hard switch to her walk, when she heard sexy eyes say in that rich baritone voice of his.

Fanita Moon Pendleton

"Shit, that Shaun ass trying to have her customers passed the fuck out."

Both men laughed again because Young said that shit just like Smokey from Friday did when Debo got knocked out. It never failed that Young and Ozone had a good time when they got together to kick it. After a couple of more toned- down drinks and more laughter, they made their exit from Club Drizzle. Young dapped his boy up and made his way to his low key Navigator, and headed home to his family.

The laughter they shared on that night helped Young through many nights in his own personal hell. Ozone was the little brother he never had, and the knowledge that his own son ended Ozone's life still weighed heavy on Young. He understood why Lil' Young put his murder game down, but it didn't make the loss any easier. Staring straight ahead, he tried to concentrate on the music as he moved forward. Thinking about the loss of Ozone had to be pushed to the back of his psyche. All of the loss that had occurred in his life had to be pushed to the back, even the loss of Lil' Young. There was death that he still needed to hand out, but there was also money that still needed to be made. Young intended to do both very soon.

Both men locked eyes as Young made his final approach towards the back table. The stare from each was intense. Life had hardened both men beyond redemption. Young was aware of the relationship Blood forged with Lil' Young. He took over as the father figure Young was unable to be to his son. There was no way that he could ever repay his old friend for that type of loyalty.

Fist Full Of Tears: The Sequel

The smile that creased the corner of his lip, making an already handsome Young look slightly debonair, broke the ice between the old friends. Blood stood up and put his arms out for a pound. The old friends gave each other dap and a heartfelt hug. It was like the years melted away. Both men pulled back and just stared at each other.

"Man you got old," Young chuckled as he pointed towards Blood.

The sound of hearty laughter could be heard as Blood said,

"Shit I am old, but still the flyest nigga you know."

They continued to laugh as Blood struck an old school jail pose. Young had to admit he missed the feeling he was having right now; the kinship, friendship, brotherhood. As the men sat down a waitress appeared from out of nowhere with a bottle of Henny, and a glass. Young looked at Blood who smiled and nodded towards the glass. A loud bass drop came from the speakers and some people started moving towards the dance floor. Young let the smooth taste of the golden liquid coat his throat as he was thinking where to start. Blood beat him to it.

"Shit is fucked up right now, huh bruh? I mean Deuce is out there, and we gonna handle that, but I'm talking about you and Lil' Young." Blood shook his head as he watched his best friend's head moving up and down and continued. "He's just like you though; stubborn, smart and deadly."

Blood smiled as he said that. He could see Young was listening intently. "When Holiday first brought him to me, all I could think about was how much he looked like you and I vowed to keep him safe and teach him how to protect himself."

Young held his hand in the air stopping Blood from continuing. He didn't want his friend to continue without knowing how much he appreciated the way he took care of his seed. Not only making sure he was safe, but making sure he was trained in the way that he would have done himself. Many niggas talk about loyalty and how hard they are, but Blood showed and proved he was a true friend, and that shit was real.

"Hold up Junior, yeah I called you Junior, nigga." They both smiled. "I know what you did for me and my seed. That shit is real and I thank you for being a real nigga on that." The sentiment was genuine and both men slapped hands across the table as Young continued. "Both you and Holiday held me down. We are forever family for that shit right there." Pouring himself another drink both men let that sink in.

Blood broke the silence as he scooted his chair closer to the table and leaned forward.

"Nothing would make a nigga like me more happy then to see you and Lil' Young work this shit out, but I'm gonna move to the side and let y'all handle that shit.

Fist Full Of Tears: The Sequel

I love y'all both and a nigga kind of feel caught up, but I know this shit will work itself out. Holiday agrees with me. He down in DC with that terrorism training, but he is clued in to what's going down with us. I'm more concerned with how we gonna handle this bitch made nigga, Deuce. Who you got rocking with you on this and how are we 'bout to move?"

The question was a valid one. Young had to put his family issues on the back burner right now because a war was brewing and he had to be on top of his game. Dealing with matters of the heart could get you fucked up and that was out of the question at this point.

Deuce had violated everything when he let pussy lead him to murder. True, Young knew he was wrong for putting the dick to Meisha. He couldn't even act like it was something that was planned or she was somebody he just had to have. When he thought about it, the shit just happened.

He went over to check on Meisha because Deuce was out of town. He wanted to make sure shit was straight over on that end; that's the type of shit family did. He remembered Meisha seemed upset about shit so he decided to stay and see what was going on with her. They sat down on the couch and Meisha began telling Young about how fucked up her and Deuce relationship was. Young just listened and let her get the shit out. She talked about his relationships with other chicks, the side chic's Deuce thought she didn't know about. She told Young she got calls several times from them. Meisha said she always told them they could have Deuce.

Fanita Moon Pendleton

For the most part Young recalled just listening and not saying much. It really wasn't his plan to get in the middle of married people's shit; hell, he had his own marital problems. But Meisha seemed to feel better just being able to vent so he didn't see any harm in letting her. It wasn't until Meisha told him about the verbal, emotional and now physical abuse she was enduring, that he started feeling a certain kind a way. The shit fucked with him more than he wanted to admit. Young grew up around abusive families and saw how that shit tore people up. He got up and went to the bathroom, just needing to separate himself for a minute. When he returned what he saw was Meisha butt ass naked on the couch with her legs spread and her eyes closed. She had her fingers deep in her pussy; he could hear her juices from where he stood.

He stood there for a minute watching as the monster in his jeans was fighting with his zipper. Involuntarily, he began to lick his lips. Young was quiet as he watched her move her hands deeper into her pleasure zone. Young knew she never heard him come back into the room. Slowly he knelt in front of her spread thighs; he could smell the sweetness of her sex. He licked her the length of her finger while it was still inserted deep inside. The warmth of his breath took over her juicy pussy just as he began to devour her sweetness. Young went harder after he heard the scream that came from Meisha. The waterfall that was released from her palace was evidence of her pleasure. He ate her pussy until she shook like a volcano. A slight smile crossed his lips when he heard her begging for him; who was he to deny her? They relocated to the rug in front of the fireplace in the 69 position. Young continued to feast, but to his surprise, Meisha gave as good as she got.

Fist Full Of Tears: The Sequel

She clamped her jaw muscles together and the juices of her mouth formed a warm cocoon around his thickness. Despite himself he began moaning into her pussy from the pleasure. He pulled her up as though she didn't weigh a thing. He looked deep into her eyes; he could tell she was catching feelings, but the lust he was feeling at the moment overshadowed his common sense, especially after Meisha straddled him with the juiciest pussy he had ever felt. It was one thing to taste the waterfall, but to feel it cascade around his dick was something totally different. He watched her as she started off with a slow grind like she was getting used to his thickness. Young made sure to push his dick to the hilt. He knew just by looking at her she wasn't used to a big dick. Meisha planted both feet firmly on the rug and took the dick like a champ. The sounds coming from Young were evidence he was enjoying the pussy he was getting.

He grabbed hold of her hips and began power fucking her. In one swift movement Young flipped Meisha over, threw her left leg on his shoulder and dug deep in her guts. He had to admit the pussy was good, but that's all it was, pussy. He wasn't feeling Meisha like that, nor was he willing to destroy his marriage and friendships over her. All of these thoughts were running through his mind as his body began to shake and he yelled out "fuckkkkkkkk Ja". His body may have been with Meisha but his mind was at home with his wife.

"Yo Young, Young." Blood tapped on the table to get Young's attention. He could tell Young was deep in thought about something, and that was understandable with all the shit that he has been through.

Rubbing his hands over his head, Blood thought *somebody is about to feel some pain and soon.* Just as he was about to call his name again, Young put his glass down and said,

> "I'm with you Junior. I was just thinking about the night that started all of this shit; not shit I can do about how shit went down."

Blood could sense the intense feelings coming from his oldest friend on this earth as he continued.

> "I lost a good woman behind my bullshit, I can't get that back. But what I can do is make the nigga who greenlit my family pay with his fucking life, and I put that on everything."

With that Young took his glass to the head and drowned it. The drink symbolized death. It was time to get down to business.

> "I got a plan," he said as he stared into the darkness of the room.

Fist Full Of Tears: The Sequel

A Mad Bitch is a Bad Bitch

Sitting outside of Club Drizzle in her royal blue Range Rover, she could feel her body temperature heating up. With her hand on the steering wheel, she twisted them back and forth attempting to transfer her anger. Watching Young walk into the club without a care in the world was almost more than she could take. She couldn't believe after all they had been through he could so easily push her to the side. She saved his life, nursed him back to health, fucked and sucked at his command and gave herself to other men, all to solidify her position in his life; or so she thought. There was a loud sound that caused her to jump slightly. Stranger than that was when she realized the sound was her banging her head on the steering wheel.

I have really got to get myself together. Maybe if I can reason with Young, he will see he needs me in his life. A slight smile came across her face as she convinced herself that this was the course of action she needed to follow. Getting her courage under her, Monica jumped out of her SUV heading towards the door she saw Young disappear behind.

Monica, or to some she was known as Dream, had blossomed into the quintessential diva with Young's help. Her gear was flawless, her body was banging, and her confidence was off the charts. Her only problem is she was crazy in love. A light haze of smoke greeted her entrance into Drizzle. The music was playing at a low volume and women were everywhere; some with barely any clothes on and some looking like they were coming from church.

Fanita Moon Pendleton

Monica was stylish in her black, grey and white snake printed Roberto Cavalli jeans. The six-inch heels added to her already model physique. Her shoulder length hair swung from side to side as she swung her neck and placed her shades on in the dark club. She found a spot near the corner of the bar, attempting to remain inconspicuous. She put the *I don't want to be fucked with face* on which immediately began to work, as she spotted men turn the other direction. Shaking her head at their foolishness, she pushed her shades down slightly and watched Young take a seat next to Blood. Monica knew exactly who Blood was. He was one of the men who Fist admired most, next to his father. She knew Blood was a stand-up dude who didn't mind putting a bullet in ya ass. Looking from man to man she thought *he might be a problem.* She didn't have a plan other than to make sure Young knew that she needed him. As she watched the two men talk, her mind was spinning. She needed to come up with a game changer and fast.

Fist Full Of Tears: The Sequel

Stack 'em Up!

There was no way to deny the beautiful woman that entered the club. He watched her from a distance thinking, *now this is the type of bitch I needs to be trying to holla at while I'm in town.* He noticed she was wearing the hell out of those jeans and her legs seemed to go on forever. Licking his lips, he had to force himself to focus on the task at hand. Turning his attention back towards Young and a big dude who he now knew was Blood, Stacks was ready to take niggas out right here and now. Talking in his ear piece he said,

> "That bitch ass nigga in here with the big ape looking nigga. I don't see why we don't just end this shit right now."

He knew Deuce was listening intently on the other end of the ear piece. The music in Drizzle switched to a tune a lot of people seemed to like because there was a rush towards the dance floor. Static could be heard in his ear as he watched the table closely and monitored his surroundings.

> "Naw Stacks. I want to get at all those bitches at one time. They need to know Deuce was the wrong nigga to fuck with. I'm about to paint this whole fucking city red," Deuce spit with venom.

He was at his mansion looking for Meisha. Anger already boiling over because she wasn't home like he told her ass to be, he said,

Fanita Moon Pendleton

"Stay on him Stacks; let me know where he goes. It's about time for us to wreck shop."

Stacks was shaking his head as his cousin finished yelling in his ear. He knew Deuce had a lot going on besides the rage of a disloyal team; he was also facing the hatred of a disloyal woman. Stacks understood that type of anger. Checking his surroundings, he noticed the beauty was still in her spot near the bar, he was stalking his prey. Stacks couldn't explain the warm feeling he was getting watching her. It had been awhile since he felt something like infatuation. Sure he fucked bitches on a regular, but he didn't let any of them get close to him. Frankly he didn't trust chicks anymore, that's why getting any type of feeling for this chick was taking him off guard. *Shit, let me focus on this nigga. Bitches will have you slippin'.* Stacks thought it was strange certified killas like Young and Blood could be caught slipping at a club. Hell, that's exactly what happened to Young ten years ago, so one would think he would be better prepared. Young smoothly pushed his chair back from the table, causing both men to stand. Stacks watched as they shook hands. He wondered what they were saying to each other, silently curing himself for not bringing his directional mic into the club.

Both men began to make their way out of the club. Stacks blended in with the women who were near him while keeping an eye on both men and the beautiful woman. She turned to leave directly behind Young and Blood. There was no need for Stacks to move quickly as he had already placed a GPS device under the left tail pipe of Young's Maserati Ghibli. He had to admit Young had good taste, because that car was a masterpiece.

Fist Full Of Tears: The Sequel

Too bad he wasn't going to be around to put it on the road much longer; maybe I will keep that for myself, Stacks thought as he turned to make his exit from the club. He watched as the beautiful one drove past him following behind the elegant sports car, and smiled; not sure if the smile was for the Maserati or the beautiful woman following it.

Fanita Moon Pendleton

About Last Night

Fist was sucking nipples so succulent he thought he would melt. He had begun to look forward to the squirming coming from underneath him. He loved the innocence she possessed countered with more sex appeal then he had ever seen a woman embrace. In the week since the sit down with his father and brother, Fist was confronted with emotions he wasn't prepared to face. He wanted to revert to what was comfortable for him… shoot everybody in his way. Joselyn has been his voice of reason.

After the sit down he headed to Josey's Bar. He wasn't even sure why; it was almost a knee jerk reaction. He felt like he belonged there each time he went to the bar and Joselyn was a big part of that. At 5'7 with a mixture of her father's deep chocolate tone and her mother's Indian features, Fist could not get her out of his mind. Hell, he wasn't even sure when she took over this much of this thoughts, but the first thing he thought to do with his mind in distress, was to go to her. Joselyn was in her normal place behind the bar giving instructions. When she noticed Fist, her radiant smile reached her eyes before her lips. Fist watched her for hours as she finished her duties. It bought him peace to do so.

During this time he played his situation over and over in his mind. He could feel the shadow before it was fully made. The smell of her perfume was causing his jeans to tighten. Looking into her smiling face, she spoke before he did.

"I get off in fifteen minutes," Joselyn smiled.

Fist Full Of Tears: The Sequel

Fist leaned back in his chair, wearing a Sean Jean hoodie. He removed it shaking his head up and down as he said,

> *"I'll be right here, ma; I ain't going nowhere without you."*

That revelation took them both by surprise; but they both understood the importance of the words. Joselyn smiled as she returned to finish her close-up routine. The bar was empty except for Scooby who was a regular. He never left before Joselyn locked up. Most people thought he was an alcoholic, but what they didn't know was he was Joselyn's cousin and there to protect her. Folding her towel she said,

> *"Scooby, I'm bout ready to lock up. You can leave now; Lil' Young is here and he will make sure I get home."*

Looking at his watch, Scooby climbed down from his stool and looked in Lil' Young's direction, giving him a strong head nod. Joselyn gave her cousin a hug and locked up behind him as she turned off the outdoor Josey's sign. Turning in Lil' Young's direction, she smiled saying,

> *"Let's get out of here."*

That was over a week ago, and since that time Joselyn has turned her heart and her body over to Fist like no other woman. As he placed her nipples back in his mouth she cried out, and that was all the encouragement he needed.

Fanita Moon Pendleton

He slipped his thickness back into her again, causing her back to arch. Fist loved the way her tightness gripped him and held him captive. He wanted to give her everything she ever wanted, but right now all he could give her was the best of him. With every stroke he hit the core of her soul. Joselyn cried out,

> "Yes Young, right there baby, right there."

Her juices could be heard with each stroke; the sound was mesmerizing. Fist lifted her leg over his shoulder and dug deeper into her soul. He whispered in her ear,

> "You belong to me. I'm gonna learn to love you the way you deserve to be loved."

Joselyn held on tight as Fist continued to brand her as his, and she simply said,

> "I belong to you." At that moment Fist felt a ripple go up his spine.

The twitching of his toes was his cue to pull out of Joselyn, but she grabbed his waist determined to keep them together as one. Looking in her eyes Fist said,

> "Are you sure?"

The look of love that stared back at him reminded him of how his mother used to look at his father. Joselyn mouth yes just as Fist let out a deep moan.

Fist Full Of Tears: The Sequel

"Ummmmmmmmmmm, yes baby, I bust. Got damn, Joselyn, shit."

Fist was still digging deep as Joselyn began to shake again while she screamed out his name.

"YOUNG!!!!" They were both drenched, but they didn't move.

They held on to each other with everything, as they attempted to regain their balance. Fist kissed Joselyn's ears, her eyes, and her nose before he rolled over and laid beside her, feeling much better than he has in a long time. After what seemed like hours, Joselyn was sitting up on her elbows looking at Young, as she continued to call him, as he slept. She wasn't sure about calling him Fist yet and he didn't seem to mind her calling him Young, she didn't like the name Lil Young. She was in awe of how handsome he was. She was mesmerized by his tiger stripped eyes; they captivated her. Joselyn didn't think she would ever let a man into her intimate space. She still had the emotional and mental scars of that fateful day ten years ago. Young broke through those inhibitions from the first time she saw him, though many men have tried and failed.

"What's on your mind?" Fist startled her with his question. He didn't even open his eyes and his breathing did not change.

Joselyn smiled down at him and said,

"I have never been this happy before and it kind of scares me." Saying the words out loud made it more real.

Fanita Moon Pendleton

Fist opened one eye and looked into her face just as the first tear fell. Joselyn has always been a strong woman. Josey saw to that. After her attack, she trained in self-defense and became an expert at every weapon imaginable, so the tears she was shedding were for her opening heart. She kissed Young on his forehead and told him her story.

> *"A month after my 10th birthday, I was walking home from school with a group of kids from the neighborhood. My friend Cathy lived in a brick house on the corner of Cypress and Linden Avenue. I lived in the first house on the corner of Linden Avenue right next to this small alley. I walked Cathy to her house; this was our normal routine. I left Cathy at her house and then turned the corner on Linden Avenue to go to home, only this day that turn wasn't routine. That turn changed the course of my life."*

Fist watched as Joselyn composed herself before she continued. There was a vacant look in her eyes, but she looked determined to tell her story.

> *"When I turned the corner, three older boys were on the corner shooting dice. They didn't even live in my neighborhood; they didn't belong on my corner. I tried to go around them but they blocked my way. One of the boys said something to me but my daddy had rules about coming straight home from school and talking to people I didn't know. I was a good girl and I always listened to what my daddy told me to do. As I tried to pass them again, one of them grabbed me from behind and placed a hand over my mouth."*

Fist Full Of Tears: The Sequel

Fist felt his hands grip the bed sheet. He didn't want to hear what she was about to tell him, but he knew in order to understand her, he needed to know what pained her deep down inside. She knew his pains. Knowing hers could only draw them closer. He relaxed his hands and reached up to wipe the tears from her cheeks as she continued.

> *"I struggled to break free, but they were strong. They taunted me and called me a stuck up bitch. They said I thought I was too good for them. Before I knew what was happening they dragged me into the small alley. I have never felt so helpless and hopeless in my life. They tried to kill my spirit as they took turns raping me, but instead they inadvertently made me a stronger woman."*

Fist was a bit confused so he asked,

> "How did they make you stronger baby? I swear I'm ready to go hunt these niggas down right now."

The look of love shinned in Joselyn's eyes. Just knowing Young's protective side included her let her know she chose well. Holding his hand to her face she continued

> *"My daddy was determined I would have my revenge. He was a member of the Young Gunz so death to them all would have been no problem. But my dad believed the only way for me to truly heal was to participate in their deaths. He trained me to be a silent killer. I am skilled in every weapon you could think of and my hand-to-hand combat skills are something of legend.*

My daddy also trained me as a sniper. When I was ready, I tracked each of the men down and one by one and issued a fitting punishment. I wanted them to suffer like I suffered. I wanted them to live with their deeds and knowledge that I could come back at any time and finish them. I blinded and castrated each of them. It brought me a peace that I never knew, but it also assisted in furthering to build my strength."

Fist was boiling inside as he listened to Joselyn tell what those niggas did to her. He felt vulnerable because he wasn't there to protect her. It didn't matter to him that the shit happened years ago, he wanted blood. It was a little comfort to know Joselyn had already taken care of the problem her own way, because he had a heart to dead their asses.

Joselyn could tell Young was agitated as she said,

"I didn't tell you all of this to get you upset, Young. I told you this so you'll know that I am not fragile. I have been through some shit and came out on top. And if you are going against Deuce, I'm riding. If you are busting on your dad, I'm riding. If the rest of the Young Gunz ain't down with you, know that I'm riding with you." Joselyn made the statement with such conviction and love all Fist could do was give her a hard nod.

He continued to watch her as she got out of the bed to fix him something to eat. He was impressed with the woman who had captured his heart. All he could think was, *I got my own ride-or-die bitch.*

Fist Full Of Tears: The Sequel

Deuce is Wild Bitches

The slamming of the front door alerted Deuce Meisha had finally arrived. He was drunk and beyond pissed. He felt like he was hiding out in his own fucking city and his own fucking house. He felt like Meisha was becoming more disrespectful since Young was alive. Deuce refused to allow them to pick up their romance where they left off. In his mind he believed they were fucking every day and laughing at him right in his damn face. The same death he planned to deliver to Young, he now planned for Meisha. Hearing her walk around upstairs, he tried to think of a time when they were happy; a time when he could envision growing old and building a family with her. Yes he was a gangster, but Meisha was his peace. More than anything, he wanted kids; a son to continue his empire, and she took that from him. Kenyatta was his son and then he wasn't. That shit fucked with Deuce. He didn't know how to handle it. The shit was driving him crazy even ten years later. At first he just wanted Meisha to suffer. He wanted to degrade her, abuse her and make her pay every day for hurting him like no one else could. But now that Young's bitch ass was back, she had to die.

Meisha walked around a home that had not been happy in years. It was one of the most beautiful homes in the neighborhood, but there was no joy in the structure. She looked around at the furnishings, the chandeliers and the marble. She now realized all that glittered definitely was not gold. Her plan was to grab some of her important papers, some clothes and as much cash as she could carry from the safe Deuce thought she didn't know about.

Fanita Moon Pendleton

She spent most of her day renting a house out in the Richmond area which was well over one-hundred miles away. She was running a fever and just wanted to get in and out so she could get some rest. Running her hands over the granite in the chef style kitchen, she knew she was doing the right thing. Meisha knew death and destruction was about to happen. She knew that Lil' Young and Kenyatta would not rest until they hunted Deuce down for killing Young and Jamilah. Taking a deep breath, she hoped her son would be careful; she didn't want anything to happen to him and she knew what a nasty bastard Deuce could be. Bowing her head, she said a silent prayer. *Lord forgive me for my evil thoughts; I want him dead more than I want anything else. He is evil personified and he doesn't have an ounce of get right in him.* Just as she raised her head and opened her eyes, she was struck with the butt of a gun. As she was falling to the ground, she heard the voice that haunts her dreams say,

"Bitch, prayer won't save your ass from me; fuck you thinkin'."

Deuce let her drop to the floor with a loud thump. Blood leaked from her head, but he was beyond giving a fuck about her. His plan now was to keep her captive so she could die with the others. He would reunite the lovers one last time as he blew their fucking brains out. He dragged Meisha's limp body into the foyer. He was amused at how her body bounced up and down as he took the two-step drop down between the kitchen and foyer. Meisha was still out cold but he hoped she felt every bump.

Fist Full Of Tears: The Sequel

He wrapped her in duct tape and then dragged her to the garage where he parked his Suburban. As he lifted her wilted body to place her in his trunk, he whispered in her ear,

"The Deuce is wild Bitch."

She misses Daddy

The fact that Monica thought Young didn't see her following him, amused him. He knew neglecting her over the last week was something he would have to deal with. Monica or Dream as some called her, learned a lot from him over the years. But the one lesson she didn't take to heart was to not to get sprung on the dick. Checking his rearview again, he could see she was keeping up with him as he entered the Indian River Plantation neighborhood. *Not really worried about Monica*, Young spoke out loud, as he turned on the Maserati voice recognition.

"Call Kenyatta."

The system quickly scanned numbers and the phone began to ring.

"Yo Pop's, what's good?" Kenyatta was smiling as he said Pop's; it felt really good to call Young his pop.

The music that was playing in Kenyatta's background was stopping Young from hearing him clearly. He figured if he didn't answer, then Kenyatta would catch the drift, so he was silent as he continued to maneuver the road ahead. Kenyatta couldn't hear anything coming from Young so he turned the radio down in his sleek grey Maserati GTS. He loved how the music reverberated from his new sound system.

Fist Full Of Tears: The Sequel

"Pop's, can you hear me?" Kenyatta said as the sound went all the way down.

"Yeah I can hear you now that you turned that noise down. That shit ain't even real music, son. I'm gonna have to hook you up with some tunes, like some O'Jay's or Maze; anything but that twerk shit you listening to." Laughter followed as Young beamed with pride at how well Kenyatta turned out.

"I like that old shit too Pop's, but you got to step ya game up if you gonna be rolling with me."

Kenyatta loved the easy relationship he had with Young. He could never feel this at ease when dealing with Deuce. His face immediately frowned as he thought about Deuce and all the pain he caused both him and his mother. That reminded Kenyatta, he never called his mother to tell her Young was alive. The week just took off and the shock was still in. He planned to call her when he got off the phone.

Young was two blocks from Willow Lawn Way. This was his chill place that only he knew about; but now with Monica following him, his peace was blown. Shaking his head, Young turned his attention back to his phone call.

"Look son, it's time for us to make a move on this nigga. Get everyone together tomorrow at noon. Let's meet at Josey's."

Kenyatta was happy to hear this. He felt like Deuce has been allowed to live a week longer than he should. The one thing that Yatta wanted was for Lil' Young to come around and work with them to end Deuce's life. A smirk came to his face as he thought TNT Underworld Syndicate could be ran by all of them together.

> "I'm on it Pop's. Have you heard from Lil' Young?" Kenyatta was really hoping the answer was yes.

Young had not heard from his namesake. He also hoped that Lil' Young would see things his way and join with him, but he wasn't going to kiss his ass. They both had the same temperament, so Young wasn't going to hold his breath.

> "I ain't heard from him and I don't expect to. But we are both after the same thing. As long as my son doesn't cross me, we're good." There was a conviction in his voice that he didn't feel in his heart as he continued. "I'm pulling in my driveway; I will see you tomorrow son."

With that, Young disconnected the call. The thought that he might have to bring heat to his own flesh and blood didn't set well with him.

Yatta could tell his pop's was in his feelings. The rearview mirror showed the concern in his own eyes. He was going to find Lil' Young and try and reason with him. *Maybe I can get him to understand that divided we fall.* Shrugging his shoulders he hoped his little brother didn't go against the grain.

Fist Full Of Tears: The Sequel

Dream Come True

Monica couldn't believe her eyes as she followed behind Young. The neighborhood they were driving through was full of over-the-top mansions. She could feel her anger beginning to boil as she thought, *this nigga had me sleeping in hotels and he had a home stashed out here.* The marble sign upon entrance said '*Indian River Plantation*'. There was a slogan that read, *The Living is Good at IRP.* The grass was greener than she had ever seen and the homes were large and spacious. It was becoming obvious Young had moved on without her. Despite this, she still held out hope. *I have never been more sure about anything in my life. I knew he was the man for me the first time I laid eyes on him.* Monica had blossomed into a very confident woman over the years under Young's tutelage. She just couldn't imagine herself without him.

Up ahead, Young slowed down in front of a large gate. He sat there for a second as the gate began to retract. Young began to drive forward into a large circular driveway in front of a stunning stone and brick mansion. There was a silhouette of a large private golf course surrounding the property. Monica's head swiveled in awe. To the right there was a four door garage with ample parking space in front of it. Parked in front of one of the doors was a sleek grey Lamborghini Aventador; it was a convertible and just as sexy as it wanted to be. Monica almost crashed into Young's Maserati looking at that masterpiece. She wanted it! She needed it in her life. She could feel his shadow as he blanketed her Range Rover. It was like her body went through a metamorphosis.

Fanita Moon Pendleton

She could feel the juices bubbling between her legs; there was a tingling down her spine, and her brain seemed to be on overload. Monica slowly turned her head until she was staring into the eyes of the man that captured her heart. She attempted a small smile, but the look in Young's face stopped her in her tracks.

> "Fuck are you doing following me, Monica?" Young had a look of disgust plastered on his face.

Monica was not going to let that stop her from pleading her case.

> "We need to talk."

She spit the answer out faster than she planned. She wanted to sound like the strong woman he helped build, but around him she was turning into jelly.

Young smirked but the light never made it to his eyes.

> "I know what you want to talk about. Follow me." With that, he turned abruptly and walked away.

Monica didn't even know she was holding her breath until she felt like she was getting light headed. *Get yourself together girl.* She had to scold herself as she stepped out of her Range Rover and attempted to catch up with Young. He was moving with brisk steps like he was on a mission. Monica was determined to make this chance count; it might be her last. Walking into the mansion was like entering a fairy tale. Upon entrance she was greeted with a massive three-story atrium.

Fist Full Of Tears: The Sequel

She walked around running her hands over things, smiling at the distinctive wood detail throughout the space. Moving down to the front living room, Monica noticed it expanded to an outdoor stone patio with nice views of the golf course. She couldn't believe Young was living in this lap of luxury without her. Her heart was screaming *as much as you have done for him, how could he?* Monica quickly talked herself out of getting into her feelings. *Don't mess this up girl. At least he let you in. That's half the battle. Now do what you do best to seal the deal.*

Young watched her from a short distance. Dream was every bit the sexy woman she appeared to be. There was no doubt she was sexy as hell, he had to give her that. He watched her hips as they swayed when she walked. Her legs appeared to keep going as if they didn't have a destination. He could feel his dick throbbing on his left leg. He didn't wear underwear because he found them restricting. The pulsating of his dick was causing his leg to vibrate lightly. Young licked his lips and began moving in her direction. The closer he got, the more he thought about that thing he taught her to do with her mouth. It was enough to make him forget he was mad with her.

"Come here, Dream," Young's deep baritone rang throughout the massive room.

Monica smiled on the inside. She was happy to hear him call her by the pet name he had given her. Young always said he saw her in his dream and that's why he gave her that nickname. Monica turned as seductively as she could in her six-inch heels. She was careful to highlight how well the Roberto Cavalli jeans were accentuating every one of her curves.

Fanita Moon Pendleton

She needed all of her magic to work for her tonight because she wanted her place back in Young's heart, and not just in his bed. There was tingling in her stomach, a mixture between nervousness and the sexuality of the moment. Young looked so good standing there Versace clean. The smoke grey sweat suit hung just right over his Versace boots. The lust in Monica's eyes couldn't be mistaken. Moving slowly in his direction, she could feel the anticipation of being held close by him once again. When she reached him, she melted easily in his strong embrace. The feeling was electric, everything she had been dreaming about. Young lifted her face to meet his and immediately sucked her bottom lip. She couldn't take anymore. Even though she didn't see the same passion in his eyes she had in hers, Monique pushed forward and kissed him with everything in her. The kiss was powerful enough to bring the most hardened heart to its knees, but would it work on Young? She didn't know, but she moved forward, at the same time reaching for the waist band to his pants.

Monica put her hands inside of his sweat pants, smiling at his famous free ball status as she stroked the monster beneath up and down. She never broke the kiss as she put the right pressure on her favorite toy. Dropping to her knees, Monica took Young in her mouth with such gusto you would have thought it was an Olympic sport. Dream was making it sloppy just like he liked it.

Young placed his hand behind her head and fucked her mouth as deep as he could. No one could compete with Dream when it came to sucking dick. *She is the best* he thought as his eyes moved involuntarily. He knew she was putting extra sauce on his dick with the hopes she would somehow suck her way into his heart. Fact is she has a place in his heart; it's just not the place she wants.

Fist Full Of Tears: The Sequel

When he met Dream she was broken; he had to build her up. There was something missing which stopped him from feeling her as deeply as she was feeling him. He needed a self-made bitch, not one he had to hold up. He needed one who could walk away from anything, including him. Dream didn't have that in her. As he pumped deeper, he continued to disconnect from Dream thinking, *good pussy is good pussy, good head is good head, but I need a Queen that can also give me those things.* Just as that last thought crossed his mind, Young shot a thick load down Dream's throat. His breathing was coming at a rapid pace as he watched her swallow every bit of his seed. That shit caused his dick to swell again. Picking dream up, Young helped her wiggle out of her skin tight jeans. He was in rare form, still breathing hard with his dick swinging from left to right. Bending Dream over in the middle of the living room, Young shoved his dick in so deep, he was sure he hit a vital organ.

Dream screamed out "Fuck me baby," as she touched her toes and threw her ass back at the same damn time. Her ass cheeks were bouncing on his thighs. Young had his strong hands wrapped around her waist. She could hear her juices making sounds as he pounded her over and over. She relaxed her muscles and accepted every inch of his massive organ. She loved the way he controlled her body. Her moans, his grunts, and the sound of the love making were the backdrop to a very erotic movie she wanted to watch over and over again. The shaking in her legs let her know an orgasm was about to cause an earthquake that was sure to be massive on the Richter scale.

> "Ohhhhh baby, I'm, I'm, I'm cummmmmmming."

Fanita Moon Pendleton

It was like Young didn't even hear her; he continued to pound the pussy through her orgasm. His breathing was like a drum beat; it was constant and strong.
Dream had to keep giving as good as she got. Before she could recover from the first orgasm fully, another one crept up her spine causing her to cry out.

"I fucking love youuuuuuuu."

Her juices spilled out of her pussy and down her legs. Young was covered in her juices and still pounding away. Dream tightened her muscles around his shaft and really started throwing ass. That did it; Young grabbed her waist tighter and yelled out

"Shitttttttttttttttttttttt girl urrrrrrrrrrgh fuck…take this nut, take this dick, shit bitch, fuckkkkkkkk."

Young shot a load of hot lava deep into Dream's womanhood. She continued to fuck him slowly, savoring the feeling of having him deep inside of her thinking, *yessss, this is my man.*

As his breathing began to return to a normal rate, so did clarity. Young shook his head at himself for getting caught up. Looking at Dream's ass still moving up and down slowly with him still inside of her, Young knew he had made a mistake. Pulling her to her feet and allowing her to get her balance, Young knew he had to let her down as gently as possible.

"Dream, we can't do this anymore. We are good together like this… when we are fucking. Hell, you are good at following through on an assignment that I give you; you will go hard for a nigga, but you are not the Queen for this King."

Fist Full Of Tears: The Sequel

Young tried to break this to her as soothing as he could, but he could see the tears welling up in her eyes as she stared through him. Then the strangest thing happened; Dreams eyes appeared to turn black.

Monica listened to Young analyzing every word he said. *Did this nigga just say I am cool for a fuck but could never be his Queen? Fuck he think he talking to. When he needed his son fucked and sucked while I kept track of him, who did that? When he needed Kenyatta fucked and sucked while I kept tabs on him, who did that? I did that for him, fuck out of here.* Dream's inner demons were beginning to get restless. She could feel her insides quiver, but she refused to drop the tears that were sitting at the surface; instead, she pulled up her clothes while never taking her eyes off Young. She watched him watching her. Their eyes were glued to each other. Dream tightened her belt as she turned away to pick up her purse. She reached into the bottom, never saying a word. When she turned back to Young, she was holding her silencer clad .357 magnum, the one he taught her to shoot. To her surprise, Young was holding his glock trained on her forehead as he said,

> "Now why you want to go do something like that Dream? We could have met for the occasional fuck, but I see you want to meet the Grim Reaper instead."

Shaking his head, Young just stared at her; *she ain't really bout this life. I took a spoiled, sheltered, homely girl and tried to turn her into a ride or die bitch. Now she thinks she a cowgirl. Fuck I'm gonna do with her ass?*

Monica started moving backwards towards the door with her gun still trained on Young. She honestly didn't believe he would shoot her, or at least she hoped. She knew she didn't really want to shoot him, but she wanted him dead. Imagine that. *I fucking gave this nigga life!* This thought sent her over the edge and Monica started busting her gun as she moved quickly towards the door. Only the baddest bitches could move in stilettos the way she was moving. She knew if she didn't kill Young he would hunt her down after this, but she was drawing the line in the sand. Monica was refusing to be thrown away like old newspaper. She didn't hear anything coming from the living room as she made her way through the door so she didn't know if she hit Young or not, but she knew she needed to get to her Rover and get through the gate before she could breathe.

This BITCH is crazy. There ain't no other way to put it Young thought as he made his way to the foyer. He had every intention of putting a bullet in Dream's ass. He had to admit he was proud of her for putting her 'G' down. It appears some of the heart he put in her might have sunk in. But no matter what, she violated and he couldn't let that pass. The blood soaking through Young's white tee only made him angrier. He swung the door open and watched her attempt to make it to her truck. Young held his glock steady and aimed towards her. Everything they went through together flashed quickly before his eyes. She literally brought him back to life. She helped him track down his son and keep tabs on him. She helped him keep tabs on Kenyatta. *Dream is a team player but her ass done played her last game* he thought as he prepared to take her life. Just as he was ready to squeeze off a shot, the light above his head shattered.

Fist Full Of Tears: The Sequel

What the fuck! Moving quickly, Young ducked back into his doorway slamming the door right before a huge blast disrupted the still of the night. The hole that penetrated the massive solid brick door assured Young he was playing with the big boys. *Who the fuck is way out here in the boonies shooting up my fucking crib!?* Young screamed over the loud sounds of bullets ripping through his walls. He was pissed with himself for being caught slipping. Shaking his head, he moved cautiously through the home being sure to avoid the shattered glass and onslaught of bullets. He thought about calling for back up, but remembered he hadn't shared his private location with anyone, not even Blood. Grabbing his AR15 out of his gun chest, Young ran to an upstairs bedroom to take the high ground. *These bitches about to find out about Young Gunz.*

She is Beautiful

He heard the shot in the distance. Stacks would recognize that sound anywhere. It was dark outside, but he could clearly see the front of the mansion from where he was perched. Using he bifocal telescope, he watched as the beautiful one ran from the home attempting to make it to her truck. She had a gun in her hand and this made Stacks smile. He wondered if she put some led in Young's ass thinking, *If her sexy ass took that nigga out I am definitely going to wife her. I need a bitch like that on my team.* Stacks watched as beautiful, long legs moved with purpose across the large driveway. It was obvious she was attempting to escape. When the large front door swung open and Young appeared with his weapon, shit got real. But that's when Stacks was at his best. He could see the blood leaking from Young's shoulder. It wasn't enough to kill him, but she did bust on him. Stacks had every intention of getting beautiful out of harm's way. He knew Young was going to go for the kill shot so he decided to show him he wasn't untouchable.

The first blast from his weapon was not intended to be a warning, but more of a prelude to destruction. Stacks watched as Young retreated, but he refused to let up the pressure. Beautiful did exactly what he hoped she would do. She double timed it to her truck and put it in reverse as fast as she could. Stacks kept the show of force coming strong. He didn't want to kill Young. There was a different time and place for that. He just wanted to play with him and allow Beautiful time to escape. The sound of crashing caught Stacks attention.

Fist Full Of Tears: The Sequel

Beautiful was attempting to smash through the entry gate with her truck. Stacks located the panel box with his telescope and took aim at it, blasting it until the gate began to retract. The screeching of tires was all he needed to hear to know that she was clear. With that, he retreated to his truck thinking, *until we meet again Young, until we meet again.*

Fist versus Lil' Young

The ringing of his phone grabbed Fist's attention. It was late but he wasn't sleep. He couldn't sleep. He was focused on his next move. Joselyn was snoring lightly, but Fist thought it sounded like music. It was the only sound right now that made any sense to him. Looking at the caller ID he could feel himself getting heated thinking *what this nigga want, he made his choice.*

> "Fuck you want nigga," Fist growled in the phone as if the scrawl on his face could be seen.

There was a slight chuckle coming from the other end of the phone.

> "What's up little brother? Save all that rah rah shit though."

Fist jumped up from the chair he was sitting in. He was normally the cool type that didn't let niggas get noticeably under his skin, but Yatta has had a way since they first met of making him want to bust a cap in his ass. He was about to really let that nigga know what the deal was when he heard it.

> "Niggas tried to kill pops tonight."

That shit made Fist sit back in his seat. He was struggling with his feelings surrounding his father. He was stuck between the world in his mind of being Fist or being Lil' Young. When he was a kid he had dreams of being able to stop the monster from killing his family. He would have done anything to have been strong enough to intervene. Hearing his brother say someone tried to kill his father was fucking with him. Young, who really just came back from the dead, still had a hold on his psyche despite what he wanted to believe.

Fist Full Of Tears: The Sequel

"Where is he?" Fist said as he reached for his glock and Timberlands at the same damn time.

Joselyn was sitting up in the bed staring at her man. She was jolted awake when Young raised his voice. His body language told her someone was about to die. When she saw him reach for his gun, she started to get up and get dressed herself, thinking, *if it's time to do battle, he's not going without me.*

Fist noticed Joselyn pulling on her pants. He nodded his head at her because he knew there was no need in telling her to stay home. She already let him know what type of chick he had by his side. It was the type of woman he needed in his corner; one who had heart and knew how to bust her gun. The training Joselyn had under her belt made her certified to run with the big dogs. Kenyatta started to talk in his ear returning his attention to the phone call.

> "Pop's is at Josey's. We called an emergency meeting. We can't do what we need to do without you on the team. It don't feel right." Kenyatta sounded serious as a heart attack.

Fist couldn't believe Yatta was saying this shit to him. Part of him didn't know how to take it. Part of him was glad his older brother had a more level head then he had right now. Another part of him had to ask the question that was pressing on his heart.

> "Does he know you are calling me?"

Fist didn't even realize he was anxious about the answer until Yatta started talking.

"No he doesn't know I'm calling you. Pop's is just as headstrong as you. Right now I have to be the one to bring us together before we let Deuce fuck our family up even more then it is. I tell you this though little brother, as much as I want us together I will fuck you up if you continue to go against the grain. So bring ya ass and stop bullshitting."

There was a pause before Kenyatta continued.

"There is nothing you or I can do about fucked up decisions our parents made back in the day. You lost a lot, I agree with that. From everything I have heard, your mother was a beautiful woman inside and out; hell, I would have loved to know her. My main goal right now is making sure the man that ultimately gave the go ahead for her death doesn't live past tomorrow. You down?"

Fist found himself nodding his head up and down. He agreed neither he nor Kenyatta could control the past and he also agreed his mother paid the ultimate price. Thinking about his mother made his heart hurt. Fist agreed Deuce had to suffer the price of a thousand deaths. His breathing was coming at a rapid pace. It only slowed down when Joselyn started rubbing his back up and down. It was like he could focus at that moment as he said,

"I'll be there." With that he hung up the phone.

He turned to Joselyn and they locked eyes. The kiss that followed was filled with passion and need; it was filled with commitment to each other; it was filled with the knowledge that somebody was about to die.

I Want Him D*E*A*D

There were remnants of duct tape still on her wrist. Meisha slowly rubbed the area that was sore from when Deuce yanked it off. Her head was hurting so bad she was sure she had a concussion. Dried blood was matted in her hair. She didn't know where she was. The room was an on-suite. There was a king sized mahogany Canali poster bed. Meisha ran her hand up and down the slick straight lines. This was the exact bed that was in their bedroom when they first were married. From the size, to the style and the color, it was an exact match. As Meisha walked around the room she noticed the Hawthorne Slatted vanity and the Maharaja dressers she handpicked prior to their honeymoon were all here in this room. She stood in the middle of the room in awe. Her mind was spinning, causing her head to hurt even more than it already did. *Am I seeing shit? Did this crazy nigga recreate our bedroom from the beginning of our marriage?* Now she knew he was crazy. Shaking her head slowly, Meisha moved towards the door; she needed to get the fuck out of there, wherever there was. She pulled and pulled on the door but it was locked. She rushed over to the window, seeing it wasn't locked. Breathing a sigh of relief, she decided not to yell out the window for help like the dummies you see in the movies. Looking down she could tell that she was on the third floor of what looked to be a town house. Her mind started to spin… *how the fuck am I supposed to get down from here without being noticed?* She turned to run towards the closet to see if there was anything in there she could use when she heard a sound that almost stopped her heart.

"You know when we first got married I truly was a happy man. I thought I had finally found the woman to be my other half; the one who would bring my kings and queens into the world to carry on my legacy."

Deuce was cool as a cucumber as he was speaking.

"You were so adamant we had to have a specific bedroom to keep our lovemaking strong and happy. You wanted this bed," he pointed towards the bed; "this dresser and that damn vanity."

He threw a bottle through the mirror of the vanity and raised his voice even more as he headed towards a cowering Meisha.

"So how did fucking one of my best friends keep our lovemaking strong and happy? How did buying all of this shit stop you from being a whore?"

Deuce wrapped his hands around Meisha's neck, pushed her against the wall and squeezed as she pleaded for him to stop. He was laughing the entire time he was choking her. The laugh was sadistic, almost creepy, and just as fast as it started it stopped. Deuce moved away from a coughing and wheezing Meisha. He didn't want to kill her yet, he just wanted to torture her and humiliate her; make her feel those things he felt by her actions. He wanted her to know before she died that she fucked with the wrong nigga.

"Strip bitch." He spit the words out dripping with malice.

Meisha was standing against the wall still trying to catch her breath. She couldn't believe she heard him right. *Did this nigga just said strip. He just tried to kill me now he want to fuck. This nigga done lost his damn mind; he might as well go ahead and kill my ass.*

"No." She said it with so much force it sounded more like a growl.

Deuce looked over his right shoulder as if someone else had come into the room. They were indeed alone, but he checked over his left shoulder just to make sure. When he turned back to Meisha she had fully straightened up and appeared like she was ready for a fight. *Well she in the right place if she want to fight cause not only am I about to whoop her ass, I'm gonna get me some of that revolving door pussy while I'm at it.*

"Bitch you forgot I will fuck you up! I can definitely help you with your memory though." Deuce lunged for Meisha with swift precession, but got a surprise because she was ready for him.

Meisha had been taking beat downs from Deuce so long she could anticipate his moves when they came straight on. She moved to the right swiftly and picked up the crystal lamp from the night stand. Before Deuce could make his next move Meisha swung the lamp and slammed it against his forehead. He attempted two more steps towards her, mouthing what looked like the word bitch. While he stumbled, Meisha hit him again with the lamp and he went down for the count. With her adrenalin pumping at an all-time high she yelled,

"I just whopped King Kong's ass."

Deuce moved a little bit which caused Meisha to jump back to reality and run for the door as fast as her sore body would allow.

She ran down the first flight of stairs almost tripping as she got to the second landing. When she finally made it to the first floor, she saw a spacious area with cocaine white couches and large fluffy pillows. The white carpet took over the room. *I got a trick for his ass.* Instead of racing towards freedom like she should, Meisha grabbed a lighter and balled up the newspaper that was sitting on the table. She burned the edge of the paper and held it up to her face as it began to burn. *Ashes to ashes, dust to motherfucking dust nigga.* Meisha tossed the burning paper on the white carpet and watched it ignite. The room began to fill with smoke. Meisha turned to head for the door as quick as she could. There were car keys on the hook by the door so she grabbed them with the intention of driving away and never looking back. She yanked the door open so fast she thought she might have pulled a muscle. The moment she stepped into the brisk night air she felt her face cave in from a punch that knocked her off her feet. All she heard was a deep voice say,

"Where the fuck you think you going?"

Who Was That?

By the time Monica checked in to the Double Tree Hotel she was shaking like a leaf and her nerves were on edge. She couldn't go back to the hotel Young had put her in. She couldn't call Fist. She couldn't call Kenyatta and she refused to bring Velnita into her dangerous world. Monica sat down on the bed and put her head in her hands and yelled, *I'm all alone.* Lying back on the bed, she replayed the events of the evening. Monica didn't plan on it turning out the way it did. She really loved Young but was not about to be his pawn anymore. Placing an extra pillow under her head, she wondered out loud *Who the hell was shooting?* That was surely the question of the day. Monica knew she would have been in serious trouble if the shooter had not shown up. There is no way Young would have let her leave without a bullet in her ass. She knew that, and if the other shooter didn't kill Young, then Monica knew her life was now in jeopardy.

The identity of the shooter was causing her distress, but in the end Monica figured maybe Deuce was behind the shooting at Young's house. She had never met him but from listening to Young and Kenyatta bitch about him, she got a good idea of what type of dude he was. She could not think of a reason Deuce would help her escape; he could have easily taken her out. She filed the information in the back of her brain. There might come a time and place where she might be able to use it to her advantage.

Monica had two choices at this point; she could either locate Young, Fist, and Kenyatta and kill them all, or she could relocate and go underground. As she laid in the hotel bed that held a mild smell of smoke, she knew living on the run was not what she wanted to do.

Fanita Moon Pendleton

She needed to come up with a plan; one that would end
with her still among the living. The bed was as
uncomfortable as her current predicament was, but that's
not the reason she jumped up quickly in a panic. The
panic set in because she realized she needed to get to her
stash of cash and weapons before Young did. All of her
stuff was in a storage unit in Norfolk. Young not only
knew where it was, he had his own key. Monica grabbed
her purse and checked her gun for bullets. Pulling her
hair back into a tight ponytail, she grabbed a hat, her
jacket and headed out the door thinking *I worked hard for
that money, did shit I would normally never do. I will
definitely kill his ass if he fucked with my shit.*

Josey's

The noise level in the back of Josey's bar was deafening. Josey was a retired Young Gun, but he was still an active part of the team. He made sure to make a place for the Young Gunz to relax and to talk business. This was his way of staying in the mix. Josey was still good to ride out if he was needed, but for the most part he maintained his bar and kept his ear to the ground. The bar was large and held all of the comforts of home, from the couches that lined the walls to the two 60" flat screens that adorned the walls. For most of the Young Gunz, Josey's was their home away from home.

Wanda Lee was standing in the front of the room, like normal, attempting to bring some order to the room of rowdy men. She was more vocal then Juice, but they were both the current leaders of the Young Gunz.

> "Check it out. We are here to hear Young out, simple as that. We all got different shit on our minds and everyone will get a chance to be heard tonight, but we are definitely going to listen to our FAM when he gets here. 'Cause that's what he is, FAM. Hell, he invented this shit that y'all been eating off of for years. Half of y'all didn't put in the work to lay this foundation, he did! So respect that or get the fuck out."

The look on Wanda Lee's face was deadly. Men were known to underestimate her and take her beauty for a weakness, but to let that caramel skin fool you would mean an instant and painful death. She was trained by Young, so her hand-to-hand combat and weapon skills were superb; and they were legendary among the Young Gunz, so no one wanted it with Wanda.

Attention was adverted towards the door as Lil' Young and Joselyn made their unexpected appearance. Kenyatta did not share with anyone his conversation with Lil' Young, not even Wanda Lee. There was an eerie quiet that fell across the room. No one knew what to expect. The word was already out that Lil' Young choked the shit out of Wanda Lee and shot Young. Seeing him walk into the room instead of being carried was a mystery to some and a relief to others. Wanda wasn't quite sure how she felt about it. She loved the shit out of Lil' Young, but she couldn't get over the fact he put his hands on her thinking, *I'm not sure how I want to deal with his ass yet, because I definitely don't play that bitch shit.* She decided she would sit on her feelings because there was a more pressing issue. *Business before pleasure.* That last thought made Wanda Lee smile. She felt like holding on to that thought would stop her from leaping across the couch and sending Lil' Young to meet his maker.

Fist surveyed the room as he made his way to the bar to speak to Josey. He knew the reception in the room would be a little chilly. He did try and choke the life from her ass, but Wanda Lee was out of line coming at him after he blew that nigga T-Mack's head off. *Fuck was she thinking? That nigga destroyed the life I had. He killed my fucking moms. How the fuck she gonna come at me about killing that nigga.* Fist had no plans on apologizing; he was a 'G' and would handle all shit like a 'G'.

"What's good Josey?" Fist dapped him up while giving him full eye contact.

Josey was wearing a half apron and a sly grin.

"Lil' Young, what's good young blood?

Young took a look around the room and matched Josey's grin saying,

> "Not sure yet old school, the jury is still out on that."

Both men shared a laugh as they settled into a seamless conversation. Neither one noticed Joselyn watching them from behind the bar. She was smiling on the inside, but refused to wear her emotions on her face. It was a skill she'd mastered over the years. Scanning the room, she noticed that Wanda Lee turned to look in Lil' Young's direction every other minute. Pouring herself a drink Joselyn thought, *Wanda Lee better not make me have to fuck her up.* Joselyn sipped her drink with one hand and felt the small of her back with the other, never taking her eyes off of Wanda Lee.

> "Glad you all could make it."

Every head in the room turned towards the sound. His voice was strong, not giving off any indication he was just in a life or death fight. Young was wearing all black everything, from head to toe. He looked deadly and debonair at the same damn time. Moving through the crowd he gave strong head nods to a number of faces that he recognized. It appeared that the entire Young Gunz team was in the house. Young was far from naïve; he knew everyone had questions. Only those who were at the warehouse got a firsthand account, now it was time to talk to the whole team together. The Young Gunz had a decision to make; either they were gonna be a family or not. There was no in between. Young was determined to rebuild the momentum of his squad and put them back on the map. TNT syndicate was imploding and it wouldn't be long before the vultures noticed the inner turmoil and attempted a takeover.

Kenyatta entered right behind Young. He looked around the room happy to see the word got out to everyone about the emergency meeting. After Young called him and told him about the attack at his house, the next day meeting was scrapped and an emergency meeting was called. Kenyatta knew the future of the Young Gunz hung in the balance. He was definitely ready to get down to business. Walking deeper in the room, he noticed Joselyn behind the bar. Moving towards the bar he made eye contact with several people. Joselyn had a shot of Hennessey waiting on him when he made it to the bar.

> "Where he at?" Kenyatta asked as he reached for his drink.

Joselyn nodded towards the end of the bar where her father and Lil' Young were engrossed in a deep conversation.

> "He's here." Her voice sounded serious and focused.

She left Kenyatta standing there looking in Lil' Young's direction.

Placing his glass back on the bar, Yatta made eye contact with Lil' Young and gave him a head nod. *Deuce don't stand a chance with all of us on his ass together.* Clapping his hands together Kenyatta was ready for some action. He didn't like the idea of Deuce running around not handled. He thought it made them look weak and he was ready to end him. Taking a deep breath, his attention was given to Young who was starting to speak.

> "Tonight that bitch ass nigga who claimed to be family tried to take me out, again."

Fist Full Of Tears: The Sequel

The base in Young's voice caused all heads to take notice. All of the side conversations stopped immediately as he continued.

> "All of you by now know what the deal is. I fucked Deuce's wife. Was that fucked up, yeah it was. Deal with it like a 'G'?, naw Deuce didn't do that. Instead he hired T-Mack, one of us, to kill my whole damn family."

He didn't raise his voice but the venom was unmistakable. You could hear a pin drop in the room while Young was talking.

> "T-Mack fucked up. He killed my Jamilah, but my son and I survived."

Fist was listening to his father from his perch near the bar. There were a flood of emotions rushing through him. Hate, hurt, love, and pain were collectively the feelings that plagued him at that moment. The loss of his beloved mother was more pain then he could deal with, but he knew he had to live. The fact that the man responsible for her death was his father caused hatred to build up inside of him, but then there was a love so strong for his father it complicated things. There was a battle brewing in his mind that he had to come to terms with. Deuce is the one who ultimately plotted to kill the entire Young family. Deuce is the one who hired T-Mack and told him to seek and destroy; Deuce was the one he needed to focus his hatred on; Deuce is the one who he needed to bring the Grim Reaper to meet, and that's exactly what Fist planned to do. He watched the strength his father possessed standing in front of a room full of certified killers, and his mind was made up.

Young saw him coming before anyone else noticed; his son, Jamilah's son. Lewis Young Jr., his namesake and the kid he loved more than life itself. No one could understand how it felt to see him walking towards him right now. Their eyes made contact. There was a lot of questions and answers in the depth of both of their eyes, but there was something else that was there as well; love. It almost felt like time stood still as Lil' Young made his final approach. Everyone now took notice and began to stand on their feet. Young reached out for Lil' Young and they embraced hard. Young whispered in his son's ear,

"I'm sorry son."

They patted each other on the back. There were a lot of emotions buried deep, but that's where they would have to stay. Right now Young and his sons were gonna stand tall. The show of strength was infectious. Kenyatta stood on the other side of Young and they faced the Young Gunz ready to shut the city the fuck down.

The Roof Is On Fire

The smell of smoke was thick in the air. The damage to the rug was contained, but the smoke had all but destroyed the living room. Meisha was tied to a chair with her mouth gagged and tears running down her face. Her right eye was swollen almost shut.

> "I can't believe he still is pinning after your skinny ass." Lynette stood in front of Meisha with her arms folded across her chest.

Lynette was pissed Deuce kept her and Lania waiting at home for over a week with not a word. He wasn't answering her phone calls, or her text messages. She decided she wasn't going to be Deuce's stepping stone anymore; she was tired. Lynette was an attorney and usually good at logical thinking, but with Deuce she was always slippin'. *I am done with his ass. He doesn't respect me.* She started packing up the little bit of shit that he actually left at her house and that's when she found it, a note from a realtor about a townhouse at 1559 Jib Court in the Fox Hill section of Hampton. Lynette already drove past Deuce's mansion, the one he shared with his wife, and he wasn't there. She envied the upscale neighborhood wishing she could give Lania this life, and Deuce was depriving her of that. Lynette staked out the Jib Court for two days. She saw him pull into the garage. He passed by her car never noticing her. She tried to think of the last time Deuce really noticed her. When Meisha opened the door, Lynette was just about to knock and confront Deuce for the last time. Seeing Meisha brought out all of her insecurities. Coming out of his hideaway spot was the woman who he wouldn't leave; the woman who he swears he doesn't give a fuck about, but here she was.

Fanita Moon Pendleton

She was wifey and Lynette was a side piece. The reality of that fact is the reason why Meisha is tied to a chair with a black eye.

> "He gave up all of this." She pointed towards her 5'9, 200lbs of luscious thickness as she continued. "He has a beautiful daughter, but he keeps running behind your bitch ass." With that Lynette punched Meisha in the face again. "Well now that you tried to kill him and burn down his house, let's see if he still wants your hoe ass."

Lynette did a search of the house after she put the fire out. She found Deuce passed out with blood streaming down his forehead. She cleaned his head up, put a pillow under him and cover over him. There was no way she could attempt to lift him to the bed. She stood over him for a while conflicted in her feelings. On one hand she loved Deuce. He gave her Lania and for that she would be forever thankful. But as she looked in his face she began to feel a sense of dread, like why did she ever get involved with this man in the first damn place. Lynette was always the woman who played things careful and close to the chest, in her career as well as in her personal life. Deuce was her walk on the wild side, but strangely she was addicted. She needed time to think so she decided to tie Meisha up and wait for Deuce to regain consciousness. Strange as it may seem Lynette hoped this would finally be the straw that broke the camel's back, and Deuce would see she was really the woman for him.

Take Yo Bitch

EZ Rental was a nondescript building on the west side of town. They had weekly and monthly rental space, which was perfect for Monica's flexible lifestyle. Her entire life was in this storage unit. She gave up her apartment once she went on her mission for Young; she didn't need it. Young promised once this was all over, she would have her own mansion to relax in. Shaking her head she remembered that promise and got pissed all over again. *This nigga played me hook, line and sinker. How could I be so fucking gullible?* She pulled her Range Rover into the parking space directly in front of her unit. She had been watching her surroundings trying to avoid an ambush, as she came to retrieve what was hers. Young insisted on having a key to her storage unit. At the time Monica didn't think anything of it. He told her it was just in case he needed to leave something for her, and she fell for it. Now she was afraid that when she opened the door to the unit, it would be empty.

There was no need to prolong the inevitable. Monica got out of her truck and raised the door to her storage unit. To her surprise, all of her stuff appeared to still be intact. She immediately ran over to a large green military trunk. Standing before it she was a little anxious. Just because all of her clothes and personal papers were still in one piece didn't mean that the things she left in this trunk were still there. As she turned her key in the lock, she didn't notice she was holding her breath until she actually had the trunk open and saw the first in her arsenal of .357 magnums. Smiling and running her hands over her weapons, she looked at the roof of the trunk. Rubbing her hands over the satin covered roof she began to pull the corners back. Piles of shrink wrapped money packs fell into the trunk almost causing it to overflow.

Monica couldn't contain her excitement. She immediately began filling her extra-large Gucci duffle bag with money. The smaller Gucci was filled with her weapons and ammo. She was all smiles that her shit was where it was supposed to be, but serious as she packed. She knew she still had to come up with the perfect plan. Monica was feeling a little jumpy, an uneasy feeling started to invade her senses and she didn't like it.

> "You're even more beautiful from the back then you are from the front."

Monica jumped on the inside but you would never know it by watching her. She spent on a dime with her baby glock aimed for the strangers head. To her surprise, standing near the storage opening was pure sexual chocolate. There wasn't any other way to describe him. He was tall, dark and handsome and the dreads hanging down his back made his swag go from zero to one hundred real damn quick. All those thoughts were going through her head as she straightened her aim saying,

> "It will be a shame to kill something so sexy." There was a slight smirk on Monica's face as she nodded for the stranger to move back outside of her storage unit.

Stacks raised his hand in mock surrender as he watched the beautiful one do her thug misses routine. He thought it was the sexiest thing he had ever seen. As he walked backwards, he licked his lips watching her handle herself.

> "I swear I have never seen anything more beautiful than you. A thug in skin tight jeans and stilettos. Umm umm umm. That's why I had to save your beautiful ass from getting shot." Stacks wore a cocky grin as he watched recognition creep into her eyes.

Fist Full Of Tears: The Sequel

Monica never let the smile show on her face, but she was happy to put a face to the action. She wanted to know for sure who was behind the shootout at Young's and now she knew. But that didn't change the fact he obviously followed her and that made him dangerous. Now that she marched him back to the middle of the driveway in front of her storage unit, Monica aimed her gun away from his head and aimed it towards his crotch figuring a gangsta is more likely to talk if you are about to shoot his dick off. Even in death, he is thinking with the wrong head; Young taught her that. Shaking her head she realized all the things he taught her over the years would stay with her for the rest of her life, unlike him.

> "You have one chance to tell me why the fuck you are following me. After that I'm done, and so are you." There was no doubt she was serious.

Stacks licked his lips like a LL Cool J. replica. He could almost guarantee her panties were soaked. She could play cowboys and Indians with the fellas all day, but at the end of the day he could see the lust steaming from her head. He stared at her intently as he thought to himself, *I'm gonna fuck the shit out of her. But I want her for myself so this is just another reason to kill that nigga Young, because he still got her heart and you already know I don't share.*

> "Look beautiful, I'm gonna kill your boyfriend; he's a done deal. You either fucking with a dead nigga or a 'G', let me know what you wanna do."

Stacks licked his lips again and put his hands down. He felt like he played her cops and robbers game long enough; she wasn't new to this. He was TNT syndicate and so was Young, so any bitch fucking with a nigga from TNT already knew which way the gun smoke blew.

Monica had a look of confusion on her face. Normally she was good about playing stuff close to the chest, but she was feeling a mixture of curiosity, sexuality and appreciation. Besides, something about the look in this dudes eye made her feel comfortable. Internally she processed that he said... he was going to kill Young. She thought to herself, *this just may be what I need right now because if I know Young, he is not finished with me.* Monica lowered her gun and placed it in the small of her back, never losing eye contact with the handsome stranger.

> "I'm Monica. Count me in." With that she turned to retrieve her duffle bags never letting the stranger say a word.

Stacks liked her style. She was no nonsense, but it wasn't bread in her, it was learned. There was still a vulnerable woman underneath the exterior and he wanted to know that woman. It was time for him to let someone get close to him again, but this time he promised himself she would be worthy of being his. Right now Monica was looking like a contender. As she attempted to walk past him to get to her truck, he held out his hand

> "My name is Jericho, Jericho Longfellow."

He caught the recognition when it hit her eyes but again, he admired how she played it cool. Stacks was taking stock of all of her qualities. He grabbed both of her bags and proceeded to place them in her trunk. It tickled him that she just stood there looking a little unsure of what to do next, but he decided to put her out of her misery.

> "Monica, can you let him go, or is it going to be a problem? I need to know now; I don't want any surprises from you." He closed the trunk and waited for her to answer.

Fist Full Of Tears: The Sequel

Monica stood next to her truck not sure if she fully knew what this man wanted from her. She spent ten years assuming shit and didn't want to start that again. Folding her arms over her shoulder she decided to put shit on the table.

> "I know who you are. I mean, I don't know exactly who you are, but I know you have to be kin to Deuce somehow. I know what's going on between Deuce and Young, and that shit is only going to get worse. What I don't know is what you want with me and how this shit is going to go down. So when I said count me in, I'm letting you know I am down for any plan that has the outcome of Young's death. To answer your question, he is already gone, I just need him dead."

There was coldness to her voice as she finished. The chill was evident and Stacks liked that shit, shit made his dick brick. He refused to deal with any weak women again. He wanted a bitch that was resourceful and not scared to bust her gun. Stacks wasn't the type of man to beat around the bush when he saw something he wanted. That shit was for suckas. He was a man of action and right now, he was ready to take Young's life and take his bitch.

Game is Twisted

Yatta slammed the phone down on the island in his parent's kitchen. It wasn't like his mother not to answer her phone. Anytime he called her, she would drop whatever she was doing to see about him. *Some bullshit is going down, I can feel that shit.* As the thought crossed his mind the inside of his hand started to itch. Now some people might think this meant they were about to come into some money, but Kenyatta knew it meant somebody was gonna die. Pacing around the kitchen, something just didn't feel right; there was a smell in the air that was familiar to him. His eyes were drawn to a stain on the kitchen floor. Bending down Yatta was getting a bad feeling. He was familiar with the stain he was seeing. It was a rusty brown color and gave off the metallic smell that was tickling his senses. Still in his crouched position, he noticed the small droplets leading to the foyer. Standing to his feet, he slowly followed the droplets with a feeling of dread as they led him to the garage. Looking around he blew out a breath of relief when he didn't see his mother in the garage. The small blood drops stopped where Deuce normally parked his Suburban.

There was a sound coming from the house; it sounded like someone moving around. Kenyatta grabbed his glock from his waist and took position near the side of the door. He hoped it was Deuce returning to the house because he was in the right mind to fuck his world up. *I know his bitch ass did something to my momma. I swear I'm gonna bleed him slow.* Whoever was in the house was obviously creeping. Yatta decided to make a move on them before they made it to the garage. He slowly made his way towards the garage door that led into the house. When he opened the door he found himself looking into the barrel of a Ruger SR9.

Fist Full Of Tears: The Sequel

"I almost blew your damn head off, nigga."

Fist smiled as he lowered his gun.

"Yeah right man, I was about to bust one off in your ass real quick. I thought you was that bitch ass nigga Deuce."

Yatta put his gun away and slapped hands with his brother before he continued.

"I think this nigga got my momma. I see dried blood in the house and shit. It's a murder game right now, on some real shit. We got to figure out a way to draw that nigga out yo."

Fist was in agreement with his brother; Deuce had to go. He was killing people over pussy, beating and terrorizing his wife, and he even tried to kill a son he raised since birth. Shaking his head he thought, *next time I see him it's instant death, believe that.* Moving back into the house, Fist had an idea. Turning to make sure Yatta was following him, Fist said,

"Bruh, I got an idea on how we can get a message to his bitch ass without even knowing where he is." Fist held eye contact with his brother.

Yatta heard the surety in his little brothers voice, but wasn't sure what the plan could be. He could see in Lil' Young's eyes he was dead ass serious. Shaking his head up and down slowly he answered, "What cha got?" He watched as Lil' Young held his hand up and started moving towards the front door. Yatta stood their looking confused as Lil' Young left the house. Yatta looked around his parent's house trying to keep his anger intact; he knew his mother's safety depended on him.

Fanita Moon Pendleton

Fist came back in the house carrying a large, brown duffle bag. By the way he was moving the bag appeared to be heavy. He walked past Yatta and placed the bag on the kitchen island. As he began unzipping the bag he made sure that Yatta was with him. Fist began to pull out stacks of military grade, C-4 plastic explosives. The olive color blocks had a shiny film and adhesive tape on its surface. He could tell his brother was confused so he began to explain.

> "A lot of bad shit done went down in this crib. The bullshit with our pop's and Meisha started here, the abuse of your mom continued here, and Deuce degraded you everyday up in this bitch. But to Deuce, this big ass mansion is a symbol of who he is. I say we blow this motherfucker up; I guarantee you we won't have to go look for his ass after that."

Kenyatta had a smile as big as day on his face. He hated the fuck out of this house. The only reason he ever stepped foot in it after he was grown was because of his mom. Most of his memories of being in the house were traumatic. He will never forget the one time he confronted Deuce when he was fifteen years old, and got a broken arm out the deal. Shaking his head as he smiled he thought *yeah... let this bitch burn to the motherfucking ground.*

> "Man, hell the fuck yeah; let's do it!"

Kenyatta started reaching for what appeared to be a cord when a voice that he almost didn't recognize stopped him in his tracks.

> "Don't touch shit you don't know shit about unless you want your body parts to end up in in the next damn town."

Fist Full Of Tears: The Sequel

Fist was dead ass serious as he looked at his brother with a deadly look. He moved away from the island deciding to get Yatta's hyper ass away from the explosives.

> "It takes a lot of training to work with explosives." Holding up a cord he continued. "This is a detonating cord and these at the end are called detonating clips. This square thing here is a booster."

Fist was holding the cord and watching Yatta to see if he was getting it. Since he was looking confused Fist said,

> "Let me handle the explosives and you stick to driving, cause you gonna get us dead as hell."

Shaking his head, they both burst out laughing. Fist left to plant the C-4 around the house while Yatta went to clean out the safe. It took about twenty minutes to plant the C-4 around the grounds of the mansion. Fist loved this shit; he was in his element. Subliminally he was killing Deuce, and that shit was bringing him a certain amount of pleasure. He felt he was somehow bringing some type of closure for his mother so she could finally begin her transition to rest in paradise; but in order to allow her to fully rest, he had to watch the life drain out of Deuce eyes. On everything, he was going to make that happen. Going back into the mansion to grab Yatta, he saw three large duffle bags in the middle of the foyer.

> "Yo fuck is all of this? You moving out this bitch."

Fist had a slight smirk on his face as Yatta walked back in the room with a duffle bag across his shoulder.

> "Oh you got jokes. Open up that bag though." Yatta picked one of the other bags up, and headed towards the door.

Fanita Moon Pendleton

When Fist bent down to open the bag, stacks and stacks of hundred dollar bills were bulging out. His smile was broad, not because there was so much money; he wasn't new to money. He was smiling because another way to kill a nigga is to take his dough. Closing the bag, he grabbed the two bags and headed for the door. Yatta was already in his car ready to roll. Fist jumped in his ride and they both pulled away from the mansion for the last time. They passed multi-million dollar mansions all of which held secrets of their own. The secrets in this mansion took out half of the block as the explosion rocked the silence of the night. But these type of secrets can't be destroyed with just a blast, they need a bullet.

Shit Just Got Real

Deuce opened his eyes very slowly. There was a sharp pain in his head as he still lay on the floor. As he reached around to attempt to get up, he felt a sharp pain in his back. *Fuccccck! I'm gonna beat that bitch's ass.* Deuce's attention was taken away from his aching back as he noticed the burnt smell in the air. *I know this bitch did not burn up my shit.* He made his way to his feet despite the pain, and started heading for the door. When he opened it, Lynette was standing on the other side.

> "What the fuck are you doing here Lynette? Where the fuck is my hoe ass wife?"

I really can't believe this nigga just asked for that bitch even though she tried to kill his ass. That was the thought running through Lynette's mind as she stood there looking him upside his head. She could feel herself begin to sweat and that only happens when she was pissed. Her breathing became labored and she couldn't hold it together anymore. Lynette threw her hands in the air and yelled out.

> "I'm over it! This bitch tried to kill you and burn your motherfucking house down and all your lovesick ass can do is cry for her ass. Well you know what, fuck you and fuck her, I'm out this bitch. Lania and I don't need you or this twisted shit you got going on over here."

Lynette stepped back. She wanted to hurt him; she wanted to make him feel the way he continued to make her feel. Before she could turn to leave, Deuce lunged towards her and grabbed her around her neck. He had a look of hatred spread across his face as he squeezed tightly. He was sweating and spit was coming from his mouth as he talked.

> "You bitches got Deuce all the way fucked up!
> Y'all fucking niggas and passing kids off as mine;
> threatening to take my fucking daughter, fuck is
> wrong with you bitches!"

Deuce ignored Lynette's attempt to free herself from his
grasp as he continued to berate her.

> "I don't know what the fuck is wrong with you!
> Your hoe ass knew I was married when you gave
> me the ass, so stop with your bullshit or Lania
> will lose a mother today." Deuce released her and
> stepped back, but he never lost eye contact with
> her.

Lynette fell to the floor holding her neck. She couldn't
believe Deuce just tried to choke the shit out of her. He
was disrespectful and uncaring but he had never put his
hands on her before. The water falling from her eyes
were not just tears of fear, but tears of pain. There was a
pain in her heart at that moment, but what he said next
sent a pure chill down her spine.

> "You my bitch. You gonna always be my bitch;
> that's what you sign up for when you fuck with a
> 'G'. Now go get my daughter and carry your big
> ass home." With that Deuce pushed past her and
> headed downstairs.

Action News 10 was blasting from the 60" smart TV
mounted on the wall. Deuce entered the room ready to
kill. He began to survey the damage to his rug and
furniture, cursing as he walked through the room. When
he noticed her tied to a chair with duct tape, he stopped in
his tracks. He looked around the room to see if Stacks
was there, but when he didn't see him it began to dawn
on him that Lynette did this.

Fist Full Of Tears: The Sequel

A slight smile crept to the side of his mouth as he thought *she might be worth keeping around if she know how to have her nigga back like this.*

Meisha was scared. She knew Deuce would make her pay for getting the better of him. The tears were falling uncontrollably as he approached with a sinister look on his face. She looked around the room hoping beyond hope someone would come and save her. Meisha was scared she might actually die this time. Her stomach was queasy and she couldn't help the bile that began to spew from her mouth.

> "Fuck is wrong with you? First you try and kill me, and then try and burn my house down and now your ass is throwing up all over my fucking white rug. You a disrespectful ass bitch, I swear." Deuce was yelling at her as he began removing the duct tape so she could go clean herself up.

As he was finishing the last piece of tape, he could hear the reporter talking about an explosion in a multi-million dollar neighborhood. Both Meisha and Deuce turned their attention to the screen as their neighborhood took over the screen. He cut the last piece of tape and moved towards the television with Meisha on his heels. He could feel his blood pressure rising as he listened to the reporter interviewing his closest neighbor. *That nosey bitch is glad to be on the news telling every fucking thing she thinks she knows.* The reporter went on to say the homeowners didn't appear to be home and no bodies were found.

Meisha was standing in front of the TV with her hands over her mouth crying. She smelled like vomit and sweat and she had to piss, but there she stood next to her husband.

She could feel his anger seeping into the air and she knew that wasn't good for the city, because it could only mean death. Her mind went to her son and hoped he was okay. Just then the front door flew open and in walked Stacks. He was still the sexiest chocolate man Meisha had ever seen, with long dreads flowing down his shoulders. She had met her husband's cousin on a couple of occasions when they visited the west coast.

> "Cuz, what the fuck happened in here? The house smells like stale smoke and piss. What the fuck is going on?" Stacks walked towards his cousin with Monica on his heels.

Deuce was still staring at the news broadcast that displayed "Mansion Explosion" at the bottom of the screen. He heard his cousin, but he didn't want to miss a word of what was said by the reporter. He needed all the clues he could get as he got ready to make a move. Stacks came and stood next to him and watched the news.

> "You think its Young?"

Stacks asked after the commercial came on.

> "It ain't nobody but his bitch ass. It was a wrong move on his part though; I'm about to send his ass back to the grave." Deuce was rubbing his hands together as he spoke.

Meisha was in the guest bathroom next to the living room. She snuck away while Deuce and Stacks were engrossed in the news. The chick that came in with Stacks was staring at her hard, but she didn't say a word. Meisha cleaned herself up as much as she could. She turned the water down low so she could hear what Deuce and Stacks were talking about.

Fist Full Of Tears: The Sequel

She knew anytime they got together some shit was about to go down. Her hands flew to her mouth when she heard Deuce say Young's name. At first she thought he was talking about Lil' Young, but when he said he was going to send him back to the grave, she knew he meant her Young. *But how can that be; Young is dead. Is he saying Young is not dead!! What the hell is going on?* She burst out of the bathroom without even thinking and yelled with tears in her eyes.

"What the fuck are y'all talking about? Young is dead! What are y'all talking about?" She couldn't control the tears that were falling from her face. Her body was shaking as she stood in front of Deuce and Stacks, seeking answers. The chick that came with Stacks was now standing looking at Meisha as if she was ready to pounce, and Lynette was standing by the stairs looking at Meisha like she was ready for war. The room was spinning and Meisha found herself getting sick again, so she ran back into the bathroom and slammed the door.

Deuce was unbothered. He was more concerned with their next move as he said, "Fuck that bitch. She the cause of all this shit in the first fucking place. But I'm about to put some wild shit in the game. Go grab that bitch."

Stacks went to grab Meisha while Deuce turned towards Monica. His look was menacing as his distrust for chicks was at an all-time high.

"And who the fuck are you?"

Monica, not one to back down, was looking at Deuce like he had lost his damn mind. *This nigga must think my heart pump kool aid* she thought, as she gave him the same look that he was giving her and said,

> "It would be a huge mistake to get me mixed up with these silly bitches you got up in here, so don't." Monica gave him a sinister smile never losing eye contact, while moving her hand smoothly to the small of her back thinking *it ain't nothing to bust this cap off, so he better chill.*

A deep baritone laugh broke the silence in the room. Deuce and Monica turned to see Stacks holding Meisha tight.

> "So I see you two have properly introduced yourselves." Stacks nudged Meisha towards the couch and told her to sit in a stern voice.

Pointing towards Monica, he continued.

> "Monica is going to make a solid addition to both our team and mine. She knows this nigga Young better than you since she has been with him for the last ten years; we can use that knowledge. Plus she's wicked and we need that spice, 'cause these bitches we got are pitiful."

Stacks laughed again as he pointed to towards Meisha and Lynette, who hadn't moved from the stairs.

Deuce turned towards Lynette almost as if he forgot she was there. He gave her a look of death and said,

> "Go get my FUCKING daughter and carry your ass home."

Shaking his head he turned back towards Stacks. But before he could start talking, Meisha jumped up from the couch and lunged towards Monica, hysterical and screaming.

"Bitch, bitch you were fucking Young!"

Stacks stepped back and put his finger up to Deuce to stop him from breaking anything up. When Meisha made it near Monica, she was met with a two-piece so tough Mike Tyson would be impressed. Meisha hit the ground Monica kicked her in the side. Monica never said a word, she just went to work. She was finally pulled back by Stacks before she could do more damage. Monica was wrestling out of his arms trying to get back to Meisha who was making her way off the floor and still attempting to move in Monica's direction.

"Meisha, sit the fuck down before I let Stacks release that 'ass whooping in heels' back on your stupid ass," Deuce yelled.

Lynette had seen enough. She was already out the door when she heard Deuce yell. She didn't want any part of what was going on around him; she had finally seen the light. Right now all she wanted to do was get to her parent's house, pick up her daughter and get as far away from Norfolk as she could. She knew Deuce would come after her, but she had to try and save her family. She got in her car as fast as she could and made a beeline for her parent's house.

Playing for Keeps

The street was quite in the suburban Chesapeake neighborhood. The houses were all cookie cutter replicas of each other. The large two-story homes reminded him of a "Leave it to Beaver" episode from the 70's. Blood had to chuckle to himself remembering the old white show, thinking *my household was so fucked up as a kid it had me wishing I was one of them little white boys on that damn show.* The abuse Blood and Holiday suffered at the hands of their father was never far from his mind. There was no one on the streets as he exited his vehicle. He looked towards the red brick home with a sense of purpose. Young had sent him on a mission; he called it insurance. Blood liked the way Young's mind worked. If anybody knew you had to have plan B ready to roll, it was Blood. The lights in the house were dimmed but he could hear a television playing. The address on the door frame read 605 Reunion; Blood thought that was ironic. Making his way to the garage door, he pulled his mask down over his face*; show time.*

Lynette was still crying as she pulled in front of her parent's home on Reunion Street. She pulled out a napkin and wiped the fresh tears from her face. Pulling her makeup from her purse, it spilled all over the floor. She pulled her visor's mirror down as she looked at herself and took several short breaths to calm down. Her hands were still shaking, both from fear and frustration. She needed to figure out her next move because she knew things would only get worse. More than anything, she was pissed with herself. Staring at the red brick home of her youth, Lynette remembered all of the lessons her mother and father instilled in her.

Fist Full Of Tears: The Sequel

They pushed her to succeed and wanted nothing but the best for her. She excelled academically but was a failure in her personal life. Lynette knew she'd disappointed her parents, especially her mother, when she decided to have a baby without a husband. She couldn't bring herself to tell her mother that Lania's father was a married man; it would crush her. So instead she just let her think he was a deadbeat dad who ran away from his responsibility. Sometimes the look of disappointment in her father's eye was hard to miss. Lynette's parents have been together since college and were still going strong after thirty years. They wanted that for her and raised her to want it for herself. The tears were starting again as she shook her head thinking, *this isn't even like me, all this fucking crying and shit. I'm beating myself up over shit that is done. I have to get it together and think of solutions; Lania is counting on me to be strong.* That pep talk is what she needed. Lynette picked up the makeup from the passenger seat floorboard and got her face together. She didn't want her parents or Lania to be worried about her. Taking another look in the mirror she smiled at her reflection and thought *I am a strong black woman and I can get through anything.* Her smile continued as the positive talk helped her put on a brave face when she entered her parent's home.

The house was quiet and that was unusual since her father was always in front of the television. Lynette called out as she walked towards the den, where her mother was normally reading the latest book for her book club.

> "Ma, I'm back. Thank you so much for keeping my lil' munchkin. Hope she didn't cut up too bad."

 Lynette entered the den trying to appear her normal bubbly self, but was stopped in her tracks. A scream was stuck in the middle of her throat. There was a sound coming from her that sounded like a whimper as she watched a hooded man sitting with her daughter in his lap. Lania was sleep, cradled in the intruder's large arm which gave Lynette a short amount of relief. She began to look frantically around the room, feeling her heart beat racing as she said as calm as she could,

> "Where are my parents? What did you do with them?"

She was almost scared to hear the answer. If he said the wrong thing it could devastate her life forever, and that was not something she was ready to face. The eyes of the stranger were piercing through the mask. The only thing Lynette could make out was he appeared to be very tall and very muscular. Her nerves were at the edge as she watched the man stand with her beautiful angel in his arms. Lania didn't wake up; she just curled up on his shoulder and snored lightly. That was the only thing keeping Lynette from attacking this brute of a man who broke into her parent's home and did Lord only knows what. In her head she was thinking *I'm so sick of these niggas I don't know what to do. I am fed the fuck up.* Lynette's nerves were shot and the stranger had yet to speak. He was just standing there holding her most precious gift and looking at her. He didn't brandish a gun or make loud threats; he didn't have to. He had her undivided attention.

> "Have a seat."

Blood nodded towards the chaise closest to where she was standing. He smirked to himself because he could see her brain moving.

Fist Full Of Tears: The Sequel

They always tried to over think shit. Blood had seen it
more times than he could count. The sound of his voice
was calm and strong as he said,

> "Whatever you're thinking, don't. Your life is
> mine now, to do with as I want. Have a seat."

It wasn't a request. The underlying venom in his tone
made that clear. Lynette moved slowly to the chaise
never taking her eyes off of the stranger. The tears she
had been trying to keep at bay had finally started to slide
down her face. She felt helpless, like she couldn't even
protect her only child. It was a pain she wouldn't wish
on anyone else. All she wanted to do was get away from
all of this chaos. She wanted to take her baby and run as
far away as she could. The ringing of the stranger's
phone caused her to jump. There was a tingling in her
spine traveling up her back and sending nervous signals
to her brain. Her anxiety was at an all-time high. The
call was short and sweet. Lynette was attempting to ear
hustle, but all she heard was *got it, see you there.* Her
brain was spinning as she thought, *got what? See you
where? I hope this nigga don't plan on taking me and my
baby no damn where.* Her face was scrunched up and she
had a deadly gleam in her eye as the stranger came to
stand in front of her, still holding a sleeping Lania.

> "We're about to leave. If you become a problem,
> this child will be motherless. I would advise you
> not to try me."

His voice held a seriousness that couldn't be denied.
Even with the mask on, you could almost guess what
expression his face held. With that, he gave a head nod
towards the front door. Lynette tried to speak but the
stranger shook his head back and forth, stopping her in
her tracks.

Making Moves

Hanging up the phone, Young was shaking his head up and down. He knew putting Blood on the kidnapping was the right move. He made sure to have an ace in the hole when fucking with Deuce. Turning his chair to face the others at the table, Young was ready to turn things up a notch. In the room sat Kenyatta, Lil' Young, Wanda Lee and Juice. This was the current power of the Young Gunz and would eventually be the power behind the new TNT. Young needed to make sure everyone was on the same page with the same vision. Staring intently at Wanda Lee, he could tell she had some shit to say. Young knew Wanda Lee and she was a beast; he trained her that way. But she was also a good ass woman, and he could tell she was hurt.

"Wanda Lee how far we go back?"

Young folded his hands on the table and looked in her eyes, as the wheels in her head spinning became evident.

Wanda Lee did a quick calculation in her head and said,

"Young, I've known you for over twenty-five years. Since you and Ozone beat the fuck out of my step daddy for what he did to me."

Her voice was full of hatred as she mentioned her stepdad. Staring at the ceiling she remembered it like it was yesterday. She was just fifteen years old. Shaking her head at the thought, she returned her eyes to the one man who she knew loved her without question.

Young also remembered that day when Wanda Lee came up to him and Ozone on the block. They were running the block for Deuce back then.

Wanda Lee was like their little play sister, always hanging around them with them big doe eyes. She swore she could be a soldier. She had grown brothers and uncles who were in the street and she admired their grind. On this particular day however, she wasn't her normal self. She walked past Young and Ozone like she didn't see them, which in itself was unusual, but when Ozone called her name she just kept walking. Young remembered running behind Wanda Lee and once he caught up with her, the blood that rushed through his body could have caused him to have a massive heart attack. Her eyes were red and one of them was almost shut closed. Young yelled for Ozone to come over to help him with Wanda. Once they were able to get her to stop shaking and tell them what happened, they were both wearing a murderous look on their face. Young told Wanda Lee to stay on the block and not to move. He and Ozone headed for Wanda Lee's apartment ready to wreck shop on her stepfather; a man who was supposed to help and support her, not try and hurt her in the worst way possible.

They climbed the steps to the dilapidated third floor apartment, both ready to get street justice for the little girl they had come to love as their own. Young held up three fingers to Ozone and counted down.
When the last finger went down Ozone kicked the door open with his size ten army boot. The hinges to the door cracked in the corner of the door frame. The home smelled of old smoke and urine. It was dark on the inside of the home and music was blasting from the rear of the apartment.

Fanita Moon Pendleton

Moving swiftly and stepping over mounds of trash and clothes, they both focused on the room where the music was coming from. Young kicked the door open and couldn't believe his eyes. This nasty ass old man was fucking a young girl from the building who Young knew couldn't be no more than about twelve or thirteen. Young and Ozone jumped on his ass like they were coming off the top rope in the WWE. The young girl was screaming and trying to get out of the bed. She scrambled and fell and scrambled again until she finally made it. She started putting her clothes on, but as soon as she turned to run out the door, Wanda Lee punched her in the face saying,

> *"Sit your trick ass down."*

Young and Ozone both stopped stomping and looked at Wanda Lee. Her eyes were black as pools; she looked empty. Young broke the silence by saying,

> *"I thought I told you to stay on the block."*

Wanda Lee moved closer to the head of the fat, blood and sweat on the floor. The determination in her movements were deliberate and evident, so both Young and Ozone slowly backed away from their victim. Young didn't move to far away but he could tell Wanda Lee was on a mission. Her stepdad was still yelling and crying out how sorry he was, and he wouldn't ever do this or that again. He began to get up from the floor slowly. When he turned and saw Wanda Lee, his apologetic demeanor switched up.

> *"You little bitch. Did you send these hoodlums in my home to beat me up? You just mad cause I want give you no dick. I'mma tell yo momma that yo' hoe ass gots to go."*

Fist Full Of Tears: The Sequel

Before he could release another word from his mouth, a shiny blade whipped across his groin area in a quick motion. The loud scream that penetrated the room caused each of the kids to run as quickly as they could. From that day on, Wanda Lee was an official part of the family even before there was a Young Gunz.

Young cracked a smile at Wanda Lee to break the tension. He knew her remembering that time was painful, but he wanted her to reflect on the fact that they were family and nothing was to come between that; not even her ill feelings about Lil' Young. Pointing between her and Lil' Young he said,

> "We all we got. Y'all all I got. Everyone in this room kept my memory alive for the last ten years. Wanda Lee I know you, so I know Lil' Young putting his hands on you has got you in your feelings."

She tried to protest but Young held his finger up and continued.

> "I already know Lil' Young feels that he was justified, because under the same circumstances and in his position, every last one of us would have done the same thing; including you Wanda Lee."

Young watched as that shit settled into everyone's psyche before he continued.

> "Right now we are in position to run everything and take that shit right out from under Deuce's bitch ass.
>
> I need to know if I am going to have any fighting among my team or are y'all gonna squash this shit. Let me know something."

Lil' Young looked around the room. He nodded at Kenyatta and Juice. When he got to Wanda Lee he gave her a wink and smiled. She smiled back at him and Lil' Young took that as both of them letting the shit go. He turned to his father and said,

"Let's do it."

With that business out of the way Young was ready to go the fuck to war.

"Kenyatta and Lil' Young, I want you to shut down all of Deuce's money houses. You more than anyone knows where they all are and how to penetrate them. I want all that shit shut down tonight."

He turned towards Wanda Lee who was staring intently.

"Wanda Lee, I want you and Juice to get the YG's and shut down all of Deuce's side hustles. I'm ready to roll because the streets are about to bleed."

Kenyatta was hype. Ever since they blew up the mansion he was ready to get the go ahead on the rest of Deuce's empire. There were seven main money houses, one located in each city; Norfolk, Portsmouth, Suffolk, Virginia Beach, Chesapeake, Hampton, and Newport News. There were smaller stash houses but they all filtered into one main house of the city. The biggest drug dealers and criminals in the city pay a hefty fee to TNT, so money was always filtering into the houses. Kenyatta knew where each house was located and who ran each house. He also knew Deuce was too vain to have already shut the houses down.

Fist Full Of Tears: The Sequel

Wanda Lee and Juice were ready to put the lights out at Razor Rims, the strip club Diva XXX, and Club Drizzle. Just the thought of shutting down Club Drizzle brought mixed emotions for Wanda Lee. For a long time, Club Drizzle came to represent the last place Young was before he was taken away from them. So every year they went there and celebrated Young's memory with a drink, and reminisce on his life. But now that she knew that Deuce was behind everything, the club left a bad taste in her mouth. Turning to Young she said,

> "Ok Young, the YG's will take care of business. What about you?"

Standing up and stretching his legs Young said,

> "I'm gonna run past the crib and scoop up my choppers. It's about to be fire in the city and I need that boss heat."

Fanita Moon Pendleton

Raid

Deuce pushed through the demolished brick door with his glock, ready to bust. Stacks and twelve of his best shooters entered the massive home and fanned out in search of something to kill. Stacks' previous calling card was very evident throughout the massive three story atrium. Walls were shattered from multiple bullet holes and glass was crushed all over the foyer and living room area. Deuce was just glad to see the damage Stacks caused to where Young laid his head, thinking *these motherfuckers got Deuce fucked up! They blow up my motherfucking shit, I'm about to blow up their motherfucking world.* It was evident no one was in the home. The shooters all began to return empty handed. This didn't surprise Deuce. He was hoping to catch Young slipping again, but in reality, he knew it was a long shot. He planned on letting Young know he was in his shit though as he said,

> "Fuck this motherfucker up. Bust up all this shit.
> Loot this motherfucker like it's a riot up in this
> bitch. That nigga need to understand that Deuce
> is about to be on his ass."

Stacks could see the fury in his cousin's face as he realized that Young bounced. There was slight amusement as he watched his shooters go about the business of making this luxury mansion resemble a section-8 apartment. Glass was shattering and wood was breaking, and it all sounded good to Stacks. He could tell his cousin had another plan up his sleeve. It was something about the look that a Longfellow had when they were about to fuck something up. Stacks knew the look well and his cousin had that look right about now.

Fist Full Of Tears: The Sequel

"What you up to, Deuce?" Stacks said walking closer to his cousin, careful to step over the broken glass and smashed wood.

Deuce looked at his cousin with a smile. There was no denying Stacks was a loyal motherfucker. He dropped everything just because his family needed him. Deuce had to respect that. This was the loyalty he expected from Young, but instead Young fucked his wife and put a bastard child in her. Young took something away from him and for that, he and everything he loved had to die; well that was the plan. Shaking his head he thought, *I put that nigga down wit' getting this money at the same time I put my own flesh and blood down. On everything, this nigga and every fuck nigga that rock with him got to get it.* There was no denying that the pain was still fresh for Deuce.

"Stacks, dis nigga got to go. He not even fit to breathe the same air as me no mo'. I got another way to get to his bitch ass, let's bounce."

Deuce looked around the mansion at all the damage his team caused and felt a little tingle inside. He wouldn't quite call it happy or even satisfaction, but he knew the time was coming that all debts would be paid in blood. He watched as some of the shooters headed for the front door, some carrying expensive items they had coveted. The unmistakable sound of gunfire could immediately be heard coming from within the house. People were hitting the floor, grabbing weapons and taking position to return fire; however, no one knew who was shooting.

The inside of the mansion sounded like world war three had been declared right in the middle of the lush green gardens of Indian River Plantation for the second time. One of the shooters was laid out in the doorway, body riddled with holes.

Fanita Moon Pendleton

There was no time for emotion or condolences; there was only time to bust those guns. Deuce knew his team was trained for this. They wouldn't be rolling with Stacks if they were weak niggas. The shooters were moving through the mansion taking cover and trying to locate the phantom attackers. They were shooting in every direction attempting to hit what they couldn't see, but Deuce knew exactly who it was. He didn't want anyone but himself to kill Young. A sinister smile crept into the corner of his mouth as a thought entered his mind: *that nigga is mine. I sent a boy to do a man's job once before, but now a Boss will handle this shit.* He couldn't explain the adrenalin that instantly sored through his body. He spotted Stacks running towards the stairs with a chopper in his hand. Picking up his AK, he ran behind him knowing he was going to seek and destroy.

> "Stacks, I'm right behind you man. Let's get these busta ass niggas right here, right now; but if you get Young in your scope, that nigga is mine."

The deadly sound was unmistakable. Deuce had a way of making shit sound both lethal and gangsta. He still wanted to end Young's life in front of Meisha so he came up with a quick plan.

Young couldn't believe his luck when he pulled on his street. He could see the line of black on black Hummers leading up to his wrecked mansion. He laughed to himself at the sloppiness or cockiness of how Deuce was moving thinking, *fuck he been doing for ten years; I'm surprised ain't nobody clipped his ass moving like this. It will be my motherfucking pleasure.*" Judging by the five trucks, Young knew Deuce was deep. But what Deuce didn't have was knowledge of the grounds and the mansion; that is where Young had the upper hand.

Fist Full Of Tears: The Sequel

Young decided against calling in his troops. He wanted them to continue on with the rest of the game plan. Instead he decided to have some fun with these clowns. Stashing his **Maserati in the** boat shed adjoining his property, He moved swiftly through the outskirts until he came upon a black steel door you wouldn't know was there unless you knew it was there. Built into the concrete and covered by light brush was a sleek fingerprint access keypad. Placing his fingers on the appropriate spaces, he watched as the door lifted swiftly. This little hideout was the selling point of the mansion for Young. He was told the previous owner was a movie star who used this secret access to keep his comings and goings private. Young had another idea in mind when he entered the hideout.

Inside he had a stash of almost every weapon one could imagine. There was enough fire power to start and end any beef. He also had undercover access to the inside of the mansion that allowed him to target the hitters while leaving them blind. He moved swiftly from one position to the next, firing precise shots with his Tech 9. He hit several of them as they made their way towards the door carrying his shit, before moving in stealth mode towards another location. Young watched as the hitters scrambled around shooting at a ghost, they had no idea what was hitting them. What he didn't see as he conducted a symphony of destruction, was Deuce. Looking through his scope, he continued to pick off the remaining hitters while searching for the real object of his affection.

While Young was moving between positions to continue to pick off the hitters as they attempted to locate the deadly shooters, Deuce and Stacks were working on a plan of their own.

Fanita Moon Pendleton

When they made it to the top floor of the mansion, Deuce pulled Stacks to the side and said,

> "They want to play hide and go seek and shit. I ain't got time for no games. I want Young, so let's go get him."

It was plain to see Deuce was on a mission. Stacks motioned for him to notice the area that the most recent muzzle flash was coming from as he watched one of his finest men fall below. The unmistakable reddish glow was a dead giveaway. Shaking his head Stacks couldn't believe Young or his people would be so careless thinking, *don't they know that the brightness of the flash can give away a shooter's location? That's sniper training 101, fuck they thinking.* Regardless of why they were moving sloppy, Stacks planned on taking advantage of the lapse in judgment. Nodding for Deuce to come up from the left flank, Stacks moved through the right flank as the closed in on the shooter.

Young saw the shadow of him coming long before he got close enough to cause any damage. He laughed on the inside that Deuce was so predictable. *I know I taught him better than this.* He let Deuce creep a little closer as he continued to shoot below causing as much damage as possible. At the last minute he swiftly turned with his Tech 9 pointing high and said,

> "Drop the chopper Bitch ass nigga!" There was a venom in Young's voice that would wake the dead.

From behind him, Young could hear the unmistakable click of a glock and a voice that was barely above a whisper; not because he was talking low but because there was a lot of emotion in his words as he said,

Fist Full Of Tears: The Sequel

"You drop your shit you fuck boy!"

Stacks appeared in front of Young with his weapon at the ready as Deuce came up from behind, hands shaking so bad because he wanted to let the bullets end the discussion. Young looked from one man to the other knowing he had fucked up. He decided against shooting his way out. He knew if Deuce wanted to kill him right then, he would have just shot. Placing his Tech 9 on the marble floor he looked at Deuce and said,

> "What the fuck you doing in my house wit' yo' bitch ass." The look of defiance Young held was running from the tip of his head through every inch of his being.

Deuce held the smirk of a man who accomplished a goal that had eluded him for years. He liked the fact that Young still thought he was in control. This would make peeling back his skin so much better. Shaking his head as he stood near Young, Deuce loved he was still kneeling on the floor in his one knee shooters stance. He aimed the gun at Young's head and said,

> "When I am done with you, the whore and your bitch ass sons, y'all motherfuckers will wish for death and I will gladly provide it to you."

Stacks was playing the back and watching the shit unfold, with his glock trained on Young just in case he decided to grow a pair of balls. He watched as Deuce placed his gun to Young's head, barely holding his emotions together. After he told Young that he would gladly provide death to him and his sons, Deuce crashed his glock against Young's head, knocking him out cold. Young's body crumpled to the marble floor and Deuce just stood over him with this look on his face that could only be described as insane.

Who The Fuck Are You, Really?

It had been hours since Stacks left her to babysit the dumb chick. Monica knew exactly who Meisha was and meeting her in person only made her believe even more that she was a stupid ass bitch. First there was the issue of turning on her husband by sleeping with one of his best friends, and then by bringing a child into the world and attempting to raise him as another man's child. Monica didn't feel sorry for the predicament Meisha found herself in; on the contrary she felt Meisha brought all of this pain and destruction upon herself. She did understand how a woman could fall for a man like Young; hell, she was still in love with him herself if she was being honest. But looking at Meisha, she was struggling with what it was about her that brought down an empire. In essence that is exactly what happened. Once she fucked Young that put an end to one of the most powerful syndicates in the world. TNT ran all of the crime in the State of Virginia. The Young Guns managed intimidation and murder like an art form; and over some pussy, it was all crumbling down. Staring at Meisha sitting on the couch looking a hot mess, Monica just had to know.

"What about you would make boss nigga's throw it all away?" Monica stood in front of Meisha with her hands on her hips and a look of determination in her eyes.

It had been a minute since Meisha felt any sense of power or a boost of energy to her self- esteem. She knew her body was runway ready and she wore sexy like a next skin. The fact remained she had been beat down for so many years she began to question her own appeal.

Fist Full Of Tears: The Sequel

Once she met Lil' Young, or Damien, hell or Fist, or whatever the hell he wanted to be called, she began to fill like a woman again. He opened up feelings in her she had not felt since Young was alive. It didn't take her long to realize who Lil' Young was, because talking to him was just like talking to Young. But the real give away was the tiger eyes that all of the '*Young*' men possessed. Smiling, she thought about Kenyatta as a '*Young*' man, too, because that's exactly what he was and now she didn't have to hide it anymore. Meisha couldn't believe there was a possibility Young was actually alive. Just the possibility alone gave her hope. As ratchet as she looked and felt at that very moment, knowledge that Young might be alive made her feel like new money. She stood up from the couch attempting to pull herself together. Her eyes were red, her hair was matted, and she didn't smell her normal fresh self. Nevertheless, Meisha held her head high and said,

"Boss niggas fall in love, too."

She watched as the beautiful statuesque woman who had a mean two-piece stood there, obviously a little deflated. Meisha wondered how long she had been fucking Young, because she was definitely in love with him. Just the thought of another woman having him was making her kind of heated inside. She crossed her arms, hugging her chest and tried not to show her true feelings as she asked,

"How long have you been in love with Young?" There were really so many questions she wanted to ask, but this one she needed to know right now.

Monica couldn't believe that this pathetic looking woman had the nerve to think she could compete with her. She didn't discount that she had a nice body and even looked okay for an old chick, but she thought to herself *she couldn't hold my stiletto on my worst day!*

Fanita Moon Pendleton

So the thought came back to why the fuck Young would risk everything to fuck with her. He put his whole family in jeopardy just to sleep with this woman. Monica shook her head as she remembered Stacks venting about Young secretly raising a son with her right under Deuce's nose. She couldn't hold it together when she realized that son was Kenyatta. Monica knew there was something about this woman for Young to risk so much for so little. Jealousy was an emotion she hadn't experienced since Young transformed her into the self-assured, sex kitten with a dangerous edge. Before Young, she was envious of every woman who appeared to have a life, because she most certainly didn't have one nor did she know how to get one. It was all about work and definitely no play. But right at that moment, Monica found she was jealous of Meisha. She watched as Meisha appeared to get herself together little by little. Even with her arms folded across her chest in a clearly defensive stance, Meisha looked surer of herself then she did previously. Monica decided the best way to bring Meisha back down to size is to make sure she knew Young was her man, simple as that.

> "Young and I are very much in love so you can pipe it down old head." Monica had an amused look on her face as she said it.

The laughter that filled the room took Monica by surprise. It wasn't the reaction she was going for. In fact she thought Meisha would break down, but instead she stood there with her arms folded across her chest laughing like she heard a joke between Kat Williams and Kevin Hart. As the laughter subsided, Monica could swear she saw a twinkle in Meisha's eye.

Fist Full Of Tears: The Sequel

> "So it looks like you have been mesmerized by that good dick Young got swinging between his legs. Take it from an 'old head', don't mistake good dick for love hunty 'cause they are definitely two different things."

Meisha turned towards the bar walking over to fix herself a drink. She could use something strong after all she had been through. Her mind began to wander as she took a sip of wine. *Deuce and Stacks left this little girl here to keep me imprisoned. She already proved she can whoop my ass, but if I can get to my purse over on that floor by the door, that glock will do all my talking.*

Monica felt the sting of Meisha's words, but she couldn't deny the truth behind them. She definitely had fallen in love with Young and the good loving he was giving out. But Monica knew it was deeper than that. She knew her love for Young was based on so much more, yet she would keep that to herself. Watching Meisha closely she could see that she was up to something.

> "No need in trying to be sneaky; I would lay you out before you made it two feet. Sit yo' ass back on the couch."

Watching the blood drain from Meisha's eyes was amusing to Monica as she thought to herself, *just like I thought - a weak bitch.* The slamming of the front door grabbed her attention. When she turned with her baby glock pointed towards the door, she immediately understood why the blood drained from Meisha's face. There in the flesh was Young. He was gagged and his hands were tied behind his back, but he was still every bit of the boss that always took her breath away. Deuce and Stacks were behind him with their weapons drawn trying to look like they were the ones in charge.

Fanita Moon Pendleton

The atmosphere in the room was thick. Monica had her glock trained on Young. Her eyes were traveling between Young and Stacks. Her grip on the trigger tightened and she could feel a tingling sensation in her heart.

Here was the man who she gave her life to; here was the man who showed her how to live; and here was the man who tossed her to the side like she was some bum chick he never gave a fuck about. She was still very much hurt. It was an open wound that only death could heal. She wanted to erase his memory from her heart and could think of no other way then a bullet to the head. Raising her glock higher, her eyes darkened.

In that moment Meisha didn't know what to say. She had dreamed about seeing Young again, but in her dreams they were swept away on a private jet headed towards an elegant private island. In her dream there were not any guns, and Deuce was definitely not there. From the corner of her eye she noticed a slight movement from Monica; it looked like she was ready to shoot Young. Meisha moved with a speed and strength she didn't even realize she possessed. She tackled Monica to the ground like she was a linebacker for the Eagles. Young just made it back to the land of the living, and there was no way Meisha was going to let this bitch take him away from her again.

Monica hit the floor and her Glock fell out of her hands. She had the wind knocked out of her but she would survive. Her mind was swirling as she thought to herself *I can't believe this bitch really jumped on me for this nigga. I should have shot them both.*

Deuce was boiling as he watched Meisha tackle Monica. The look on his face as he held his gun on Young was like the devil in the flesh.

Fist Full Of Tears: The Sequel

He was in his feelings as he thought to himself *the disrespect this bitch shows me never seems to cease when it comes to this nigga. That's cool though, 'cause they can be together in hell.* Shoving Young violently, Deuce swiftly moved towards Meisha and snatched her up from the floor

> "Your hoe ass has disrespected me for the last time. Tonight you and dis nigga BOTH die."

Spit was flying from Deuce's mouth, but it was his eyes that gave away his murderous intent.

Young jumped towards Deuce swinging his leg around in a semicircular motion. He struck him in the back with the front of his leg causing him to release Meisha and fall forward almost losing his balance. They assumed Young was down for the count since they had his hands tied behind his back and his mouth gagged up, but Deuce had no way of knowing that over the last ten years, Young became a black belt in martial arts and the roundhouse kick is a Young specialty.

The moment Stacks noticed what was happening he made a move, but he was a step too slow. Young put the moves on Deuce so smooth and fast it caught them all off guard. When Stacks moved in to put his hands on Young, he was met with a Scorpion Kick to the face. It was a powerful kick, but not enough to knock a 'G' like Stacks down. He stumbled back and bounced right back up. Both Stacks and Deuce rushed Young together. There wasn't much Young could do with both of his hands still tied behind his back. He did one more kick move before he was tackled roughly by both Stacks and Deuce. They all crashed through the glass center table causing glass to fly throughout the living room.

"Son of a bitch! Urgggggggggggh!" Deuce yelled loudly as he attempted to pull glass splinters from his bleeding hand.

Young was visibly hurt; blood could be seen soaking though his tee-shirt. He was attempting to get up from the floor only making it to his knees. Stacks jumped back up unhurt and immediately kicked Young in his side and punched him in the jaw causing him to crash back to the floor. Part of his reasoning was to make sure he was subdued, but his other reason was because he saw the look in Monica's eyes. She was still under that nigga's spell and Stacks was determined to let her see him defeated.

"Take a nap bitch nigga, I'll wake you when the Grim Reaper comes for your punk ass," Stacks said through clenched teeth.

Young was down but not out. He could take an ass whooping; that wasn't shit. The fact Deuce hadn't killed him yet is where he fucked up at. Young didn't survive ten years to go out like no chump. He saw the hurt in Meisha and the anger in Monica and understood where each woman's feelings were coming from. He really had love for both women in his own way. Each of them had their own good and bad qualities, but of the two, Meisha is who he was most concerned with. She is his first child's mother and of the two women, Meisha has suffered the most for loving him. She lost any meaningful relationship with her husband, she suffered abuse at his hands, and she for the most part, emotionally raised a son by herself and did a damn good job. It gave him a sense of pride to see her stand up for him today; it showed him that through it all, she still carried him in her heart. Right now Young was just going to bide his time and wait for Deuce to do the inevitable; make a dumb ass mistake.

Fist Full Of Tears: The Sequel

I Am In Love

Riding with his brother, Kenyatta wasn't sure how to act. He didn't know if they would ever have a regular big brother, little brother relationship. One thing for sure, they didn't miss a beat when it came to busting their guns together. Lil' Young was a natural beast. Yatta had a sense of pride about it. He felt like it was in their genes or something. Neither of them was raised with Young, but they both turned out deadly and smooth just like him. Now how was that possible unless it was meant to be?

> "Don't you think it's ironic?" Kenyatta said as he turned towards his little brother in the passenger seat of his Maserati.

Fist had a confused look on his face as he shrugged his shoulders and continued to look through his binoculars saying,

> "What you talkin' about now Yatta?"

A smile crept to the corner of Kenyatta's mouth as he studied his brother's face from the side. He thought it was amazing how much he resembled their dad. On the other hand, he got more of his mother's good looks, coupled with his father's build.

> "I was just thinking that although we didn't grow up with Pop's, there is no denying his influence on us both, that's all."

When Lil' Young didn't respond, Yatta picked up his on binoculars and studied the house directly in front of them. They ran through the other main stash houses with little opposition. They saved the hardest for last. Ivanhoe Court was picturesque. It was the perfect cover for a stash house.

Fanita Moon Pendleton

The Burbage Grant section of North Suffolk was a family community with two parents, kids and a family pet. No one in the neighborhood could have suspected Denise and Robert were two of the deadliest members of the most notorious syndicate in the world. By day they had two teenage kids; a daughter who was seventeen, a son who just turned nineteen, and a dog. It was a perfect cover for an imperfect life. But when the neighborhood was sleep, they collected the daily cash from the other houses, counted it, logged it and prepared it for transport to the main warehouse. They handled any disputes that arose from any of the Suffolk stash houses. Murder was always on the menu if money got fucked up. Kenyatta knew Denise. She was Deuce's cousin. She was ruthless, even more so than Robert. Kenyatta watched her kill a whole family once. One of the house leaders fucked up some big money, mainly due to mismanagement of his runners. Denise lined up his entire family from the grandmother to the infant child. She had each member of the family kneel down in front of the house leader. He was pleading with Denise to spare his family and just kill him. Denise never talked. She never took her eyes off of the house leader as she systematically shot each member of his family in the back of the head. As he continued to watch the house, Kenyatta shook his head as he remembered the screams coming from the house leader. They were almost not human sounds as he dropped to his knees begging Denise to shoot him too.

Denise bent down in front of the man and said

> *"Perhaps tomorrow. But today, you better get me my fucking money."*

Kenyatta had seen some hard core shit since he started taking on a larger part in the family business, but he had never seen a woman put it down like Denise had done.

Fist Full Of Tears: The Sequel

That shit stuck with him and now it was time to deal with her, Yatta wanted to make sure Lil' Young knew who they were dealing with.

> "Check it. This last one might not go down exactly like the others. This bitch Denise is crazy. Don't sleep on her ass. We're in and out. Everybody dies." With that said Kenyatta put the binoculars down and checked his ammo.

It was 1a.m. when the white Benz pulled into the driveway on Ivanhoe Court. The garage door opened automatically and the Benz pulled forward. Kenyatta and Lil' Young were prepared to slip into the garage as it was closing. After some discussion, this was plan B. Fist always had plans A-C worked out. What if they parked in the driveway? What if more than one car comes home? There are too many variables. Fist learned this from Blood years ago and it had worked well for him up to this point. He wasn't use to working with a partner, and wasn't quite sure he liked it. All he wanted to do was handle this business and go catch the big fish. Moving into position, they struck as soon as the garage was halfway closed.

Aiming his **Ruger SR9 towards the Benz, Fist was the** first to speak.

> "Nice and slow, and I'll make the cleanup go easy."

Kenyatta held the other door down with his glock pointed, ready to fuck something up. He liked the way Lil' Young was handling himself; real smooth. He could tell he wasn't new to this at all. There was no way Yatta wanted Lil' Young to leave the family; Young Gunz could use his talent.

Both doors to the Benz snapped open at the same time.

"Be easy,"

Fist said as he zeroed in on the stocky figure exiting the vehicle.

"Turn slowly with your hands in the air. Don't try any slick shit you can't recover from."

The stocky figure apparently didn't hear well. When he turned, he made a quick decision to shoot his gun. It was the last original thought he ever had. The silenced SR9 sent his body flying over the opened door and crumpling to the floor. The passenger was already open and a thick, light bright, damn near white female jumped out the car running over to the fallen figure. Kenyatta held his weapon aimed at the chicks back. He was impressed with the thickness of her ass, but not enough not to lay her down next to the dumb ass nigga who got froggy.

"You gonna die with this nigga or are you gonna be easy like my bro said."

Yatta liked the fact she wasn't all hysterical, screaming and crying. If she would have been that type of chick he would have bust that ass off jump. Instead she was still knelt down next to the body, never saying a word. As she made a move to stand up, Yatta noticed her ass jiggle involuntarily, or was it involuntarily as he said,

"A phat ass not gonna save you today sweetheart. Where the fuck is Denise?"

The chick was fine, there was no denying that shit, but as Fist watched his brother work he could see she would be dead at the blink of an eye. Fist began scoping the inside of the car where he noticed three extra-large duffle bags on the back seat.

Fist Full Of Tears: The Sequel

He told Yatta to keep an eye on the bitch while he checked out the car. When he opened the first bag, it was filled to capacity with money. Checking the other bags he found them to be full as well.

Fist figured this was the collection for the day, but he wanted it all.

"Where the fuck y'all got the rest of this money stashed?" Fist didn't pull the bags out of the car. He planned on driving the money out of there.

Sexy Red still hadn't answered his question and now she wasn't answering Lil' Young. Kenyatta wasn't dealing with the disrespect. He snatched her ass clear out of her stilettos and slammed her on the hood of the car, face first. She yelped at the sudden movement, but still didn't say a word.

"I like pretty bitches who think they're gangsta, that shit gets my dick hard. But you done fucked around and ran into some real bosses this time baby. Fucking with me is like saying fuck ya life. So you either got something to say or you can get busy dying."

Kenyatta pressed the barrel of the gun at the back of her head and took a step back.

She grinned as she watched the other one staring at her with his ruger pointing in her direction thinking, *damn these niggas sexy as fuck. I know who they are; these are Young's boys. My momma told me they might be headed our way. She told me and RJ not to come back to the house, but I just couldn't leave all that damn money in the house. Momma said fuck that money just go to the down low spot. I talked RJ into coming and now he dead. If I don't think quickly, my ass gonna be dead, too.*

Fanita Moon Pendleton

"I don't know where my momma at. The money is in the deep freezer in the corner. There ain't no need to kill me." Her matter-of-fact tone was emotionless. She wasn't pleading for her life, just making an observation.

Fist checked the freezer and sure enough it was full to the hilt with money. Money wasn't new to him nor was it new to Yatta, but he couldn't deny this was a lot of fucking money. He motioned for Yatta to bring the chick over to the freezer.

"Any more money in this fucking house? If you're lying, you gonna burn in this motherfucker, so let's have it."

Fist noticed the lie before she could stop shaking her head no. Playing it off he had the chick begin to load the trunk and back seat up with the money from the freezer. He told Yatta the house had to burn and the chick with it. He knew the death of both of her kids would bring Denise out of hiding. It took over thirty minutes to empty the freezer. Never underestimate how much trouble cold money is to handle. Fist worked with the chick to clear it out while Yatta poured gasoline throughout the house and the outer area. When he walked back into the garage, he was just in time to see Fist put a bullet in Sexy Red's head. Even her head exploded pretty. Shaking his head he told his brother "Leggooo."

Fist put the Benz in reverse as the house began to smoke. Kenyatta hopped in the Maserati and they made their way out of the quiet neighborhood just as the house became engulfed in flames. Fist turned the radio up, letting Yo Gotti and French Montana's 'Work' blare from the banging Benz system.

Fist Full Of Tears: The Sequel

Kenyatta followed behind Lil' Young, caught up in the adrenalin of the night. Pushing in the lighter he lit his last blunt, turned on KEM and rode the high. The Tupac ringtone, "Dear Momma", grabbed his attention from his blunt and music. He hadn't been able to get in touch with his mother for days and was beyond worried.

Yatta knew Deuce had something to do with her not answering his phone. He regulated his breathing to calm himself down as he answered.

"Ma Dukes! Where the hell are you?"

Yatta half expected to hear his mother's feisty voice saying "*you don't even check up on your old momma no more; shame on you Yatta,*" and then burst out laughing in her loving way. But Kenyatta knew that wasn't going to happen. Even if she did magically appear on the phone, the last time he saw her she was in bad shape, mentally. Once she had to finally come clean about her affair with Young, sleeping around with Lil' Young, and Kenyatta and Lil' Young being brothers, she was mentally drained. So much had happened over the last week or so Yatta just hadn't had the opportunity to check on her. His thoughts were interrupted.

"Ma Dukes... that's cute. You were always a soft ass momma's boy. I knew you could never have really been a Longfellow. Like I told you once before, you a fuck up that I can't tolerate on my team." The disgust was felt by every word that Deuce spoke.

Kenyatta gripped the phone tight, not wanting to show Deuce that he got to him, but not being able to hold back either.

Fanita Moon Pendleton

"Man on some real 'G' shit, fuck you! I could give two fucks about your bitch ass. That's what you always been to me, a bitch ass nigga playing boss. Now where the fuck my momma at pussy? Miss me with the rest of that bullshit you talkin."

You could literally see the smoke coming from Yatta as he picked up his speed passing Lil' Young on I-464. The laughter in the phone broke through the silence.

Deuce thought it was hilarious that Kenyatta thought he had balls. Looking over at Young tied down to a chair with duct tape still covering his mouth and Meisha staring at him from the sofa with crocodile tears floating down her face, he felt a sense of purpose.

"I tell you what son of a bitch... that's what you are, right? You're the son of your hoe ass momma and this bitch ass nigga over here." Deuce paused for dramatic affect before he continued. "Yeah that's right Lil' nigga, I got yo' momma and your daddy, fuck boy. Now bring your bitch ass and your little dumb ass brother to Drizzle in an hour and we can have a fucking family reunion." Deuce slammed the phone down pissed beyond control. He didn't give Kenyatta a chance to respond.

Kenyatta was staring at the phone. He knew he heard Deuce right. *He has Pop's and Ma Dukes! Fuck!* The ringing of the phone caught him off guard, but he answered it on point.

"I will fucking skin you the fuck alive, *don't* get me fucked up!"

Fist looked at his phone to make sure he dialed the right number. Once he verified it was Yatta's number he calmly said, "What happened Yatta?"

Fist Full Of Tears: The Sequel

If ever there was a desire to kill someone, killing Deuce was at the top of Fist's agenda. Once Kenyatta told him what happened, Fist told him to meet at Josey's so they could regroup with everyone. He told Kenyatta to hit up Wanda Lee because he knew he still wasn't on her favorite person's list. Wanda Lee and the Young Gunz were supposed to be shutting down Club Drizzle, but Fist wanted them to hold off on that for a second. When they hit Club Drizzle, he wanted it to be epic.

Josey's

The screeching of tires could be heard coming from the parking lot. Not just one but several cars were pulling up in a hurry at the same time. Joselyn received a call from Fist asking her to close the bar. It took her fifteen minutes to get her regulars cleared out. She promised them one drink of their choice tomorrow. No one moaned too much. For the most part they knew the Young Gunz frequented the bar and the word on the street was some shit was about to pop off. She was standing behind the bar counting money when he came through the door. To her Young was like her breath of fresh air. The way he walked with a self-assured swag caused a small eruption in her thong. There was a serious and determined look in his eye which caused her to close the drawer and meet him in the middle of the bar.

"What do you need me to do?"

There was no need to beat around the bush, Joselyn would ride to the end of the earth with this man and right now he looked like he could use his rider.

Fist held eye contact with Joselyn as people started to filter through the door. Everyone had a deadly look cascading over them. Most people went straight to the back room but some lingered near the bar talking to each other. Fist grabbed her around the waist and pulled her close. To the naked eye you would think they were engaged in a passionate kiss or hug, but Fist was issuing orders to his rider.

Fist Full Of Tears: The Sequel

"We killing niggas or we fucking. I mean what are we doing, seriously?" Wanda Lee's words hung in the air for a second longer then was comfortable.

Fist felt Joselyn attempt to pull away from him when she heard Wanda Lee's remarks. He felt her body heat up and recognized the sign immediately. Joselyn was about ready to go to Wanda Lee's ass, but he needed her to focus on the plan, fuck what Wanda Lee talking about. Fist released Joselyn but not before giving her a strong passionate kiss that caused some to snicker on the sly.

Kenyatta walked in the door just as Fist released Joselyn.

"Yo bro let's make some moves, cause shit is all the way fucked up." Kenyatta said   moving fast towards the back of the bar.

When the last of the team took their seats Kenyatta began to lay out the situation. Once he told everyone Deuce had Young the room burst into loud conversations.

"Let's not all try and talk at once. I know everyone wants this shit dealt with and we are just the ones to do it. It's time for TNT and the Young Gunz to close the chapter on Deuce ass for good, so this is what we are going to do."

Kenyatta was sounding like the leader he was meant to be. The entire room was engrossed in the plans for the move that needed to take place in the next thirty minutes. Fist phone began to vibrate in his pocket. He stepped away from the crowd once he saw who was calling. It was time to bring the fucking heat.

Make it Drizzle

Not everyone knew Deuce was the owner of Club Drizzle. He liked to keep some of his investments close to the vest. He had businesses all over the state of Virginia and partial interest in businesses in residing states. There weren't many businessmen as gifted at making it rain as Deuce Longfellow. He was college educated and street tested; that was a dangerous combination. If he was honest with himself he would say it was time to let this shit go. Deuce's ego just couldn't handle the deception heaped against him by his wife and one of his best friends, a man he considered family. The strange part was Deuce was smashing chicks all over the East Coast, and had been doing so for most of his marriage. But he refused to allow the same to be done to him without some repercussions.

The music in Drizzle was completely off. The quietness gave off an eerie feeling like some real gangsta shit was about to go down. On any other night Drizzle would be packed with patrons, but tonight it was completely empty. Deuce made all of the workers leave for the night and closed the business to attend to killing business. He had one of his hands bandaged from the glass that cut him earlier, and carried a crazed look in his eye. Meisha and Young were tied to chairs facing each other in the middle of the dance floor. He needed to have Young's kickboxing ass tied down. Deuce watched as tears fell from Meisha's eyes and she showed a look of concern for Young who was still bleeding from his injuries. Young smiled at Meisha since the gag had finally been removed from his mouth.

"Isn't that cute. The two of you love birds back together after all of these years, just in time to die together. It's sort of like Romeo and Juliet. They were so in love they committed suicide. And you two committed suicide the moment you crossed me." Deuce sounded amused at his analogy. He was trying hard to mask the anger bubbling in the pit of his stomach from just watching the two of them.

Cryptic laughter filled the air. Young had his head leaned to the side as the laughter continued.

"You've always been a weak nigga. I see that hasn't changed in the last ten years." Young was nodding his head up and down as if he were agreeing with himself. "When Ozone and I were young niggas, I saw your weakness. The way you're crying over pussy you pushed my way show's me you still the same pussy ass nigga."

Meisha had a worried look on her face, and she was shaking her head back and forth with her eyes bulging out of their sockets. The tears continued to flow as she watched Deuce move towards Young with his gun pointing in his direction saying,

"A pussy, huh? A weak nigga, huh? Nigga I fed you and your motherfucking family since you were a little nothing ass nigga. And what do you do? You fuck me. Nigga fuck you and everything you love bitch."

Deuce was pointing his glock towards Young with a face full of anger and pain. As he pulled the trigger, a sense of satisfaction washed over his face.

Meisha screamed out and rocked her chair back and forth, almost knocking herself over. The tears were flowing hard as she watched Young's chair fall over. She never heard him scream out because the blasting of the front door was so loud that it drowned out all the sound in the room. Meisha screamed out,

> "Help us, help us, I think he killed him." She was yelling hysterically.

Deuce growled at Meisha and pointed a threatening finger in her direction. Shots rang out as the club filled with men and women, blasting weapons in all directions. Deuce was blasting his glock back and forth as he tried to avoid being shot.

Stacks was in a discrete location inside the club and Monica was also strategically planted as well. Deuce wanted to give the illusion he was alone. He knew how the Young Gunz operated. He had been witness to many of their take downs, but tonight they were sure to be emotional and that could make them move sloppy. Stacks watched as the Young Gunz rushed the club blasting their weapons, but not trying to hit anything. He assumed they wanted to make sure Young and Meisha were safe first, but he was about to disrupt all that bullshit. Taking aim, Stacks could see a man who resembled Young make his way to the dance floor. Thinking to himself he said *that must be that nigga Lil' Young. Well he on the hit list too, so he got to go.* The feel of the shadow that loomed over him caused Stacks to move slightly to his right just as his shot rang out and went immediately over Fist's head. Stacks was immediately met with a crashing blow to the head and placed in a headlock. He was dragged from his post in the cut, struggling for his release.

Fist Full Of Tears: The Sequel

Fist was still looking around the club after his close call with having his head blown off. He was tired of the bullshit as he yelled out.

> "Enough of the bullshit Deuce. Death is here for you. I'm here. Your punk ass didn't kill me ten years ago. Kenyatta is here. Your punk ass didn't bust a nut and have him. Young is here and it looks like once again your bitch ass didn't kill him. That's what you wanted bitch ass nigga; all of us here, so now what the fuck you gonna do?" Fist stepped on the dance floor waving his gun around for emphasis.

Deuce noticed one of the Young Gunz helping Young up from the floor. He was shot but it didn't look detrimental. This caused him to simmer inside. He noticed Kenyatta and Juice dragging a belligerent Stacks towards the dance floor. It took every bit of both men's strength to handle Stacks' wild ass. Deuce spotted the sinister look Kenyatta gave him as he was making his way towards the dance floor. The look pissed him off beyond measure. Thinking fast, he reached up and grabbed Meisha roughly from her seat by her neck. The yelp she squeezed out before her trachea was obstructed was earth shattering.

> "I should have broken this bitch's neck years ago. I should have cut off the airflow to her lungs and her windpipe when I first found out she was fucking that bum. But when I found out this hoe allowed me to call this bastard my flesh and blood that was it for me. So yeah I wanted everyone dead, and I wanted this bitch's life to be miserable for fucking with a BOSS!" Deuce was spitting as he swung Meisha around by her neck.

Kenyatta dropped his hold on Stacks and ran onto the dance floor towards his mother, yelling,

> "You a punk, simple as that; always putting your hands on someone weaker than you, but I ain't a kid no more. I'm about to fuck you up." He was dropped to one knee by a bullet to his leg. The shot came from out of nowhere. Kenyatta screamed out, "Fuuuuuuuuuuck"

Everyone took cover but Deuce. He knew exactly where the threat was coming from and he silently hoped she picked them all off one by one.

Monica sat in the cut and aimed her next shot for Fist, but he had successfully hid himself behind a large speaker. She wanted all three of them dead; Kenyatta, Fist and last but not least, Young. Placing the .380 on the floor, Monica pulled out the baby AK Stacks gave her and fired several successive shots at the speaker almost demolishing it. What she wasn't counting on was the large muzzle flash the AK gave off. Her position was compromised so she quickly relocated to avoid being caught.

The large front door opened and in walked a figure that was unfamiliar to most, but not to Deuce. He was shaking his head as she walked more into the light and his face showed his distaste.

> "Lynette, what the fuck is yo big ass doing here. Where the FUCK is my daughter?"

Before she could answer, he heard the faint sound of a crying baby and a dark figure emerged holding his precious Lania.

Fist Full Of Tears: The Sequel

Blood moved forward with both Lynette and the little girl in tow. He made eye contact with Young and Fist. They both moved forward just as Blood made it to the dance floor. Young's deep baritone could be heard saying,

> "Join the party Blood. I see you brought company." He then turned to Deuce with nothing but hatred. "Whoever you got hiding in here shooting, now is the time to call them down or once again you will be fatherless. And let her go NOW!" His words could be heard through the gritting of his teeth.

Deuce made eye contact with Stacks who was being held hostage by Juice and his glock. Stacks looked around the room; he really didn't want to give up their ace in the hole. Looking back at his cousin he could see the desperation in his face. He didn't want to see anything happen to the baby, but he also knew if he got Monica to give herself up, they would lose their last bit of defense. Shaking his head at his cousin in the negative, he couldn't think with his emotion right now.

Fist saw the decision being made. He didn't know who this fuck dude was but he wasn't fucking with him anymore. Before anyone knew what hit them Fist put a bullet in Stacks forehead large enough to roll a bowling ball through. He pointed the gun towards Lynette and said,

> "The next bullet is for the kid, so let's get this show on the fucking road."

Deuce released his hold on Meisha and watched as she crumbled to the ground choking, gagging and crying uncontrollably. He looked at her in a heap on the dance floor and instantly lost it.

"Shut the fuck up. All of this is your motherfucking fault from the jump cause you couldn't keep your hoe ass legs closed."

He looked around the club at Young, Lil' Young and Kenyatta and at all the weapons pointed at him; he wanted to say fuck it and go out blasting. But then he looked at Lania and his heart gave in to his gangsta. She was only two years old and the only thing in his life that made any sense. There was no way he could let her lose her life because of his ego.

"Monica, come out now." Deuce yelled loudly, never taking his eyes off of Lania.

Monica heard him, but she couldn't believe her ears. She was shaking her head hard. There was no way she was putting herself in the line of fire because he turned pussy. She just watched Fist blow a hole through Stacks brain and she didn't want any part of it. She was actually preoccupied with trying to create an exit strategy. She never saw the takedown coming. Before she knew it, she was kicked in the face by a stiletto boot.

Young knew he heard Deuce correctly when he said Monica. He watched as Lil' Young looked around the club with anticipation after hearing the name as well. He wanted to be wrong so badly, but after the incident at his mansion it all made sense. Looking from Lil' Young to Kenyatta, he had a feelingthis wasn't going to end well.

Wanda Lee was forcing the chick towards the dance floor by gun point. She didn't know who the hell this chick was, but judging by the astonished looks on the faces of Young, Lil' Young and Kenyatta, she knew some shit was about to pop off.

"Dream, did you motherfucking shoot me? Fuck is wrong with you?" Kenyatta's verbal attack came as soon as she stepped on the stage. There was a mixture of anger and surprise in his voice.

Monica ignored him as she made eye contact with Young. There was no denying he still held a presence and she was trying to place the look in his eye. She didn't know if it was surprise, anger, or… just then she thought it might be the look of a man who didn't want the other shoe to drop. Monica laughed inside because she was about to make that motherfucking shoe do the stanky leg.

"Well if it isn't Fist and Kenyatta. Damn y'all looking good. Did ya miss me?" Monica had an amused look on her face.

Deuce was looking confused. He scratched his head and yelled out loud as he looked at his cousin lying on the cold, dirty dance floor with a bullet in his head.

"Bitches! You just can't trust these hoes. Now how the fuck you running with my cousin and at the same time you on a first name basis with the enemy?" Deuce was noticeably fuming.

Monica held an amused look on her face at Deuce's antics. She could see how it might look from his perspective, but she didn't give a fuck. She did everything Young asked her to do and at the end she still got fucked, so if she was about to go down, she was gonna have her say. Looking back and forth between the three men of her affection, she noticed the deep level of hate that was sent her way from each man for his own reasons.

"To Fist I am Dream, to Kenyatta I am Monica…but to Young I am the woman who he sent to fuck you both." Monica caught the surprised looks on everyone's face as she continued. "So while y'all were falling for me, I was falling for a boss."

Young was still bleeding profusely from his gunshot wound. He walked slowly to the middle of the dance floor and slapped the shit out of Monica causing her to drop to one knee.

"You running with these niggas? You trying to kill me bitch?" His anger was boiling over.

Meisha couldn't believe this bitch was fucking Young, Kenyatta and Lil' Young. She wanted to slap the shit out of her too. She already didn't like the bitch because she knew she was fucking Young, but now to learn she was fucking Lil' Young and her son was turning something in her already queasy stomach. Watching Young slap Monica only made her wonder if he really had love for this bitch. Young was never violent towards women so for this woman to evoke this type of emotion in him made Meisha wonder. Her mind was going a thousand miles a minute as she watched Monica attempt to get back up from the floor.

"No need to put yo hands on me Young. Everything I did was for you. I loved you enough to suck both your son's dick. I loved you enough to fuck them on demand. I would have done anything for you, BECAUSE I LOVED YOU you dumb son of a bitch," Monica said as she stood to her full strength.

Fist Full Of Tears: The Sequel

Kenyatta was watching this shit with an unbelievable glint in his eye. There stood the woman he asked to move to Virginia with him; the woman who put that pussy on him so good he was gonna make some changes in his life for her. Even once he found out she was fucking his little brother, he still wanted her. He was just letting things cool off, but always had plans on finding her. But right now, seeing how deep the deception went, he wasn't sure how to feel. Looking at Lil' Young and then looking at his Pop's, all he could do was shake his head.

> "This shit is whack. You send this bitch to give me pussy, what's that shit all about?" The look Kenyatta had on his face was more of disappointment then anything.

The two men shared a look. Kenyatta was hoping to see in his father's eyes a look of redemption, but what he got instead was a cold vacant stare. Loud clapping refocused everyone's attention. The Young Gunz were all standing around the dance floor still pointing their guns on Deuce, all ready to blow him away at a moment's notice. Fist was looking around at Young, Kenyatta and Monica as he clapped.

> "To say I am not surprised is an understatement. Young has made it apparent he don't give a fuck about nobody but himself. I really don't give a fuck for real. I'm here today to get justice for my mother, who was much too good of a woman to be mixed up with you disloyal motherfuckas." Fist eyed his father with nothing but pure hatred in his eyes as he continued. "Dream, you won't nothing but some good pussy to me, so fuck what you talking about. You and Young deserve each other."

Turning towards Deuce his voice got louder.

> "You are the real reason I am here." Raising his gun he definitely got Deuce's attention. "What you took from me, I could never express how deeply you scarred me. If it wasn't for that loyal nigga right there holding your baby, I would have been all fucked up in the game. But he held me down and I can never repay him for that. You on the other hand, I can definitely repay you." The sound that rang out seemed louder than normal. Everyone knew it was a gunshot; the smoke from Fist Ruger left no mistake. Deuce hitting the dance floor hard put an end to any speculation.

Fist looked around the room at everyone as they stared back at him. The baby was screaming as if she could really understand what had just transpired. Lynette was crying uncontrollably. Fist couldn't believe this is what he dreamed about all of his life.

> "Fuck all of y'all." He pointed around the room and turned to leave.

Kenyatta couldn't believe this is what it came to. He watched as his little brother turned to walk out of his life before he could even get the chance to really develop a friendship with him. He didn't want it to end like this.

> "So you gonna just give up? Walk away from an empire. An empire that by birth right belongs to US! What the fuck is wrong with you man. Look, I know Pop's fucked up. I feel a certain kind a way right now, no lie; but at the end of the day he is OUR father." Kenyatta was pointing between himself and Lil' Young.

Fist Full Of Tears: The Sequel

Fist stopped in his tracks. He understood where Yatta was coming from but he felt his brother was reaching for a dream that wasn't possible. He knew Yatta wanted them all to run the business together, but Fist wasn't feeling that shit. He didn't trust those around him and that was bad for business.

> "By all means Yatta, you stay with these back stabbing motherfuckas. That's your choice. Me, I'm cut from a different cloth. I would rather seek my fortunes on my own then surround myself with this bullshit. I'm out!"

Fist turned to leave and Kenyatta started to go after him but stopped when he heard the forceful sound of Young's voice.

> "Let him go! He's running from himself and ain't nothing you can say to change that. I'm just his excuse, so fuck it. Deuce is dead and TNT will go on. End of fucking discussion. So run and hide like a little bitch."

Fist heard weapons chamber as he moved through the club. He didn't even look; he just knew that guns were aimed at him. He didn't put it past Young to have him shot down like a dog, so he kept it moving until he heard her voice.

Meisha couldn't believe Deuce was dead. But watching Lil' Young turn to walk out was more than she could bear. She screamed out,

> "What about ME! What about me, Lil' Young? Don't leave me here."

Kenyatta looked at his mother with a mixture of disgust and surprise. Young looked at her and began to shake his head as she continued.

"I'm pregnant! Do you hear me, I'm pregnant?" Meisha was yelling and crying at the same time. She wasn't going to raise another child by herself if she could help it.

Fist heard what she said and he couldn't fucking believe it as he thought to himself, *is this bitch really serious. She fucked my dad and had a child by him, then knowingly fucks me and expects to bring a child into this world. What the fuck does she expect from me?* Fist didn't want anything to do with Meisha or anyone that reminded him of this place. Joselyn is the only person who he would allow to remain in his life. Turning to face Meisha he was gonna let her know to do what she had to do, but count him out. Before he could say anything, a distant shot rang out. Everyone hit the ground waving their guns in every direction. The pained sound of Kenyatta screaming out filled the club.

"Momma, momma, someone shot my motherfucking momma." Kenyatta was stretched out on the dance floor holding his mother in his arms as the life seeped out of her.

Young gave a strong head nod and everyone immediately fanned out to sweep the entire club looking for the culprit. Fist knew exactly who it was. He couldn't believe it, but he had to get out of this club quickly before shit really got real.

THE AFTERMATH
1 YEAR LATER

The ICU at Norfolk General Hospital has been his mother's home for the last nine months. That's how long Meisha has been in a comatose state. Kenyatta made sure his mother had the very best doctors around. They monitored her breathing and brain activity until she was out of immediate danger. Now they could concentrate on maintaining her health, especially after her recent delivery of a healthy baby boy. The hospital was buzzing ever since Meisha was first admitted. She was transferred to Norfolk General from Sentera Leigh because they were more equipped to deal with a pregnant comatose patient. Kenyatta was by his mother's side throughout the ordeal. He had every intention of putting the baby up for adoption the moment it was born until he actually saw him. Once he saw his little brother, his heart melted and he thought about what his mother would want him to do.

It has been three months since Louis Young III was introduced into the world and his mother's prognosis had improved some. Doctors said she has improved to a persistent vegetative state. At first Kenyatta didn't know if he should feel good about the news, but the doctors went on to explain a persistent vegetative state differs from a coma because a coma lacks both awareness and wakefulness. There was so much information to grasp, but what Kenyatta could understand is that his mother could possibly open her eyelids and regain some awareness but still not be functioning regularly. He was holding out hope that this was moving in forward progress, but in the meantime he was raising his brother by himself with help from Lynette.

He couldn't believe it when she stepped forward and asked if she could help him, but he was definitely glad she did. Kenyatta in turn became like a surrogate father to Lania.

Despite an exhaustive search, Kenyatta never found out who shot his mother on that fateful date. The Young Gunz did a full search of the club, but to no avail. Everyone pretty much went back to business as usual and TNT got back on track, but Kenyatta couldn't let it go. He replayed that night over and over in his head and the one thing that stuck in his head was his little brother hurrying from the club. Kenyatta could never figure out why he wouldn't stay and try and help figure out what was going on, especially since he was just told he was going to be a father. Young told him to let it go, but Kenyatta has been searching for Lil' Young for months.

Can I Live

Can I Live by Jay Z was blasting through his beats as he bobbed his head up and down to the lyrics. Fist was feeling what Jay was saying but the hook itself was his new theme. It had been a year since he walked away from everything and everyone. Blood and Holiday both have tried to reach out, but Fist put distance between them, too. They both respected his space, but they knew how to get in touch with him for business purposes. Fist was still the best at making bodies drop on demand.

A couple of months ago, Blood called him and told him his son was born. He still hadn't processed that Meisha was in a coma, but still carrying his child. Blood also told him TNT was back on top. He said Young and Kenyatta had revamped the outdated system and increased profits 90%. Fist recalled the conversation…

> *"Blood I don't give a fuck about all that. Where is the baby, what's up with that? What's his name?"*

> *"Why you worried about that little boy, I thought you didn't want to have nothing to do with that?" Blood asked with a curious smirk.*

Fist knew Blood was fucking with him, but he let him have that.

> *"Real talk, I don't know how to feel. I know not having my daddy in my life when I was a kid fucked me up. I guess I'm sitting here wondering am I repeating the cycle of bullshit my father started."*

"Oh okay, I feel you. Well Louis Young III is with Kenyatta. He and Deuce chick that has the little girl are raising him. Looks like Kenyatta has really been holding his mother down, but he hasn't dropped the hope of finding who shot her."

Fist hung up the phone after that. He never told anyone he knew who shot Meisha. He would take that shit to the grave with him so Kenyatta can forget that. Even so, he would protect Joselyn to the end of the world and back. She was only at Drizzle because he told her to hang back as the sniper just in case he needed her. She would have never been there if not for him. Once she heard Meisha say she was pregnant, it was only pure jealously that made her take that shot.

Fist mind drifted back to when he left the club that day as the music continued to blast in his Beats.

Leaving the club, he could still hear Kenyatta yelling out. He was yelling for someone to bring the truck to the front so they could get her to the hospital. Fist moved through the parking lot, jumped in his car and peeled out. He headed straight for Josey's and prayed she was already there. His heart was beating at a fast pace because he wasn't sure if she had made it out of the club, but when he pulled into the parking lot, he could see the grill of her truck on the side of the building. When Fist walked into the bar, Josey was coming out of the back room with a pissed off look in his eyes. Once he spotted Fist his look became even darker as he said,

Fist Full Of Tears: The Sequel

"What the fuck have you got my daughter into?"

Fist tried his best to soften his approach because he knew Josey was just worried about his daughter.
        "Where is she?"

He moved past Josey as he asked the question, and went into the room Josey had just left. There with her head on the table was Joselyn; his beautiful, sweet, feisty Joselyn.

Joselyn looked up when she felt the figure looming over her. She smelled his cologne and her nerves started to calm some. She looked into his worried eyes and said,

> *"I'm sorry Young, I don't know what came over me. I have never felt like that before."*

Fist grabbed her gently and took her in his arms.

> *"Don't you apologize to me. This entire situation was fucked from the beginning. I am leaving; the only thing I need to know is if you are going with me?"*

The door burst open, almost coming unhinged as Josey stepped through the door.

> *"Hell naw she ain't going with you. What the fuck is going on here? What the fuck did you do to her? Josey was in full protection mode and ready to put Lil' Young to sleep behind his baby girl.*

Joselyn ran to her father. She needed to calm him down because he was known for blowing a gasket.

"Daddy, I have to go. I did some shit that if it comes out, will put our family in danger and I can't accept that. I love you too much to think my actions caused harm to you. Don't be mad at Young; this one is on me and my jealousy. Young had nothing to do with it."

She could feel her father's breathing begin to regulate. She turned to Young and said

"When do we leave?"

An hour later they were on the road. The only thing Joselyn took with her was her needed identification, pocket money and access to her big money. Other than that, they would buy stuff later.

The song in his ear switched to a slow groove bringing his thoughts back to the present. Joselyn was sleeping soundly and Fist was thinking about his son. He didn't know where this paternal instinct was coming from all of a sudden. He didn't think he was capable of it to tell you the truth, but part of him was feeling that his son should be with him. Slamming his head on the table he couldn't help but feel like he was letting his son down just like his father let him down. Fist decided he was going to get his son.

The next morning he packed a duffle bag with clothes and weapons. He turned to see Joselyn sitting in the bed staring at him.

"You got a job?" She asked as she stretched.

There was no need to not tell her what was going on with him, especially since his mind was now set on bringing his son back with him. He told her about the call from Blood and that his son was living with Kenyatta and Deuce's old girlfriend.

> "I am going to get my son and bring him back here to live with us."

Fist watched her closely as he let this information soak in as he continued.

> "I know this may seem sudden, but it's been fucking with me for a couple of months. It just don't set right with me to have a son out there and not be in his life. I grew up with that shit and it fucked me up."

Joselyn jumped up from the bed and walked across the room. Her head was spinning; she didn't know what to think or what to do. She kept in touch with her father so she knew Meisha was in a vegetative state. She knew before Fist when his son was born, she just didn't know how to tell him. She wasn't sure if she was in the right mental state to be someone's mother, but she didn't know how to tell Fist this without him thinking that she was selfish. She loved Fist and wanted to support him. She grabbed her duffle bag and started throwing clothes in it.

> "What are you doing baby? I need for you to stay here and get the house ready for my son."

Fist put his bag down and took Joselyn in his arms. He could see she was shaking so he asked,

"What's going on baby? Talk to me."

Tears she didn't even know were ready to fall began to fall like a water faucet. She could only guess that her nerves were shot as she said,

> "I don't know how to say this without sounding crazy. I feel so guilty for how this is playing out all because I was jealous of Meisha. I'm not sure if I should be the one helping you raise her son." Joselyn let her head fall onto his chest.

Fist held onto her tight and rocked her slightly back and forth. He knew she carried a lot of regret over the last year, but he wanted her to let it go. Right now he needed his right hand chick on point.

> "Fuck all that Joselyn. I need you on point with me right now while I do this. I don't know what type of shit these niggas gonna try and pull when I go get mine. But if shit pop off, I need to know that you won't hesitate with that trigger." He lifted her head to look her in the eye and said,

> "Are you with me?"

Joselyn was moving her head up and down as she took a deep breath. She decided right then to stop feeling sorry for herself and get back to being the rider her man needed. She finished packing her backpack and met Fist at the door, as they got ready to make the long drive back to Virginia to get his son.

Virginia is for Lovers

If you would have asked Lynette a year ago if she would ever be in love again, she would have unequivocally said "no." She closed her heart to love because the last time she opened it she almost got herself, her parents and her child killed. She will never forget when she made it back to her parent's home after she left Drizzle. Blood had already told her her parents were alive but they were tied up in the bedroom. She took her sleeping child from his arms, ran as fast as she could from the club and jumped in his car and headed back to rescue her parents. When she entered her parent's home, it was eerily quiet. She put Lania down in her car seat and rushed to the bedroom. There on the bed were her parents looking bugged eyed at the door as she came through.

> "Momma, daddy, ohhhhh I am soooo sorry. I love you. Are you guys okay?"

Lynette ran to the bed as she was talking and crying. She untied both of her parents and hugged them hard.
Her mother was crying with her and hugging her, while her daddy wanted to know what the fuck was going on. Lynette helped her parents get themselves together, and then they all sat down and talked. Lynette will never forgot that day. For months she found herself having PTSD moments. Lania saved her sanity. Caring for her everyday stopped Lynette from slipping deeper into depression.

One day she was at the hospital with her daughter visiting her god sister who was in a terrible car accident in the downtown tunnel. She had severe and life threatening injuries and was admitted into the Intensive Care Unit.

Lynette wanted to believe bringing Lania to visit her would be the therapeutic break that was needed to heal her body. The visit was one sided as usual, as Lynette brushed her hair and read a book to her. Lania slept through the visit, which was just as well. There was a loud commotion in the hallway; a man was yelling over another man, trying to talk. Lynette walked over to the window and pulled back the curtain just as the man yelled,

> "Every day I come in here and y'all tell me the same shit. No one knows what the hell they are talking about. I want another opinion." Kenyatta was in a heated argument with his mother's head doctor.

Lynette put her hands over her mouth. She recognized the man instantly. She would never forget any of them. She remembered how devastated he was when his mother was shot. She wanted to reach out to him then like she wanted to reach out to him now. Common sense took over and she closed the curtain and went back to her friend. A week later Lynette was at the hospital and decided to stop by and visit the woman who she had disrespected so much by sleeping with her husband. She couldn't believe she had been that type of woman. In a small way, she felt like she owed Meisha something. She walked over to her and smiled at how peaceful she looked lying in the bed. Lynette bowed her head and said a silent prayer for her.

> "Thank you for visiting my mother. I wish more people would."

Fist Full Of Tears: The Sequel

Lynette couldn't move. She knew who it was, but she wasn't sure how he would take her; the woman who was sleeping with his mother's husband and the woman that had his mother's husband's child. She didn't think she could take a confrontation so she turned quickly and tried to run out of the room. Kenyatta moved quicker and blocked her path.

> "Stay with me." His request sounded more like a plea then a demand.

Lynette stared at him with eyes that didn't hide her fear. She was shaking a little and not quite sure what to say.

> "I don't care, do you understand? As far as I'm concerned that shit was between you, my mom and Deuce, and they both had as much to do with it as you. Right now I just want you to stay here with me while I visit. If you want to go I will understand."

They spent at least two hours that day just talking. Lynette learned a lot about Kenyatta on that day and three months later, they were inseparable. He is good to Lania and she helps him with Louis. The situation works for them both. Neither one of them expected to fall in love.

Reunited

463 Court Street was the old location of the Mansion
Night Club in Portsmouth, Virginia. Young brought the
entire building, including the restaurant downstairs. This
was the new headquarters of TNT. Blood was sure to slip
that little bit of information to Fist during one of their
conversations. Pulling up in front of the building, Fist
remembered coming to the club once when it was in its
hay day. When he entered the building he could tell a
full renovation had taken place. The restaurant
downstairs was now a huge reception area and
conference room area. It looked like the kitchen was still
active as Fist saw several people in a conference room
with food. The décor was modern with a mixture of
royal blues and gold. The large solid steel receptionist
desk was different, but gave the area a certain hip feel.
Dominique 'Da Diva' was on the radio; Fist remembered
hearing her dishing Da Daily Dirt when he was in the
area. He walked towards the reception desk and was
greeted by an older woman, who strangely didn't look
out of place in the modern office décor. Her name tag
read Mrs. Jones, and outside of the thin lines of grey in
her hair, she could easily pass for her early thirties.

> "Good afternoon, welcome to TNT. How may I
> help you son?" Mrs. Jones said in a tone that was
> genuine and affectionate.

Fist was dressed in Armani and looked every bit the
young businessman. He returned the welcoming smile
that reminded him of his mother.

Fist Full Of Tears: The Sequel

"Good afternoon, Mrs. Jones. I would like to see Kenyatta Longfellow, please."

Fist didn't notice the slight look of disgust that left as quickly as it came from her mouth. She stared at the young man in front of her for a second longer before recognition hit her at full speed. She picked up the phone in a hurry and said,

"Can you tell Mr. Young that he has a visitor, please?"

As she was hanging up the phone she saw the look of confusion on Lil' Young's face, but she didn't address it. Mrs. Jones may be family but she didn't feel it was her place. She continued to stare at him as he played with his iPhone thinking to herself *he is the perfect blend of my baby, Jamilah and his daddy. I wish I was around when all of this shit went down, but doing a twenty-year bid in Goochland Prison for Women for killing my husband, kept me out of my daughter's life. My husband had been beating me for years and I stuck in there at least until my daughter was grown and gone; but I just couldn't take it anymore. I wasn't there to protect her and my grandson, and that shit hurts me to my heart.*

The ringing of her line snapped her back to reality. She listened to the person on the other end and then hung up and got his attention.

"Ok son, you can go to that first elevator and press 1, The receptionist will help you from there. It is really good seeing you."

Fist didn't understand why the lady was being so sweet to him, but she made him feel like he should know her. He thanked her for her help and headed to the elevators. He went over in his mind what he wanted to say to his brother. Fist knew Kenyatta was pissed with him, but this isn't that. This is his need to stop the cycle and be there to raise his son. Kenyatta can either go with the plan or deal with the consequences. Fist wasn't above getting dirty and Yatta damn well knew it. The elevator opened to what used to be the second floor, dance floor, but now it was a huge lobby and reception area decked out in masculine greys and blacks. There was plush grey carpet and huge black leather sofas throughout the area, with a steel reception desk similar to the one on the first floor. Behind the desk was a man Fist recognized as a member of the Young Gunz.

> "Hello Lil' Young. Kenyatta will be with you shortly, have a seat." He pointed towards the sofa near the huge bay window.

Fist didn't like this King Kong looking nigga calling him Lil' Young. If he never heard the name again, it would be fine by him. He hated that Kenyatta named his son with the family name. He was actually considering changing it soon. Before he could get himself pissed even more, a large glass door opened and Kenyatta walked out wearing a funny expression on his face.

> "Well what do we owe this unexpected visit?" Kenyatta didn't know if he was happy to see his little brother or not. He couldn't understand. *Why now? What does he want?*

Fist Full Of Tears: The Sequel

The sarcasm was not lost on Fist but he really didn't give a fuck. He walked past Kenyatta like he owned the place, and went into the door he saw him emerge from thinking to himself *this nigga betta not play fucking games with me cause I will fuck him up in this bitch.*

They stood toe to toe, both breathing hard and neither speaking. The shit was getting old so Fist broke the stale mate.

> "I'm here for my son. I know his mother is still incapacitated and you call yourself raising him. I am coming to take him with me." Fist saw Yatta flinch when he said why he was there. The shit was comical but Fist decided to spare him laughter.

Kenyatta walked away from Lil' Young because he wanted to fucking strangle him. He couldn't believe this nigga was trying to take his little brother away from him. He knew at the end of the day it was his son, but where the fuck has he been. Kenyatta wanted fucking answers; he felt like Lil' Young owed him some truth. He had no plan on keeping him from his son. He already knew the father/son shit was personal with Lil' Young. But he wanted to know why he disappeared when his mom needed him most. Leaning on his solid oak desk and folding his arms across his chest, Kenyatta let out a breath.

> "What type of nigga are you man? You come in here demanding to take my little brother, but you walked out on his mother when she needed you most. What type of bullshit is that, man?

My mom has been near death for over a year, and WHERE THE FUCK WERE YOU?" Kenyatta was getting emotional. He really didn't want this meeting to go like this, but fuck it.

Fist shook his head at his weak ass brother thinking *those must be his mother's genes 'cause that is not a Young trait.* He couldn't figure out why Kenyatta thought he owed him an explanation.

"I'm here to pick up my son, not debate with you. Meisha is YOUR mother, not mine. She is not my wife, nor my woman. What she is, is in a vegetative state and unable to care for MY child, so the job falls to me as his father. So all I need from you is the address and time TODAY that I can pick up MY fucking child; no more, no less." There was a fire in Fist's eyes that assured anyone looking that death was imminent.

Kenyatta jumped up from leaning on the desk ready to fuck his little brother up. He couldn't believe Fist was talking like his mother didn't matter. Before he could make a move the door slammed open and in walked Young.

It's So Hard

Joselyn spent the afternoon with her father. Although she talked to him on the phone often, she hadn't actually seen him in a year. She had one more stop to make before she met up with Fist to pick up the baby. Pushing through the ICU door, she came to the room she learned was Meisha Longfellow's room. When she walked in the room, tears immediately came to her eyes. Meisha looked to be in a peaceful sleep. If it weren't for the beeping machines and cords attached to her body, Joselyn could actually fool herself into believing that she was asleep. Moving closer to the bed, Joselyn sat in the steel chair feeling sad.

Joselyn tried over the last year to forgive herself for shooting Meisha. This is not the first time she shot someone, but it is the first time she did so because she was in her feelings. She was actually hoping to tell her how sorry she was. It would finally allow her conscious to be at rest.

"You don't even know me Meisha."

She was looking at her as if she could hear her.

"My name is Joselyn and I'm the person responsible for you being like this."

Joselyn was waving her hands around Meisha's body and then pointing around the room.

"If it wasn't for me thinking you were trying to take Fist from me, I would have never shot you."

Joselyn took a deep breath, her heart was pounding but she knew she had to do this.

"I am going to help Fist take care of your son until you get better. I will make sure he knows everything about you and that we bring him back to Virginia often to visit you."

Lynette stood on the outside of the door with a sleeping baby Young. She was bringing him to visit his mother, which was her daily routine. She heard a woman talking but decided not to disturb the visit. But once she heard the woman who called herself Joselyn, apologize for shooting Meisha, Lynette turned as white as a ghost. She backed away from the door, careful not to make a sound, and immediately picked up her cell to call Kenyatta.

****

Young still had it. He was the quintessential businessman. He never let that side of him shine when Deuce was running TNT. He stuck to the gun play and let the business end be run by Deuce and Ozone. But now that he was running the show, business was really booming. Kenyatta was his right hand; turns out he liked being in the office since Deuce wasn't there. Wanda Lee and Juice still ran the Young Gunz and they were stronger than ever. Young tried unsuccessfully to bring Blood aboard, but he had his own thing going.

Fist Full Of Tears: The Sequel

Young knew that Lil' Young was a freelancer with Blood and although he should be happy, he felt somewhat slighted that his son would rather work with someone else then join the family business.

> "The Prodigal son returns,"

Young said loudly as he gave a sinister smile towards his youngest son. Young's statement referred to a character in a parable Jesus told to illustrate how generous God is in forgiving sinners who repent; the only problem is Young wasn't in the forgiving mood.

Fist shrugged off what Young was talking about; he wasn't even trying to hear it.

> "Miss me with that old man. I came for my son, not to listen to this bullshit you and your brainwashed puppet talking about. So let me know where to pick up my lil' man, and I'm ghost."

You could cut the tension in the room with a knife. Kenyatta calmed himself down and decided to let it go. He walked over to his desk and wrote his address down on a piece of paper. He ripped the paper from the pad taking some of his frustration with it. Walking over to his brother he said,

> "I'm not going to fight you on this. He is your son, and for some strange reason I feel like my momma would want him to be with you. If you don't want shit to do with us, then fuck you, too.

Meet me at that address in an hour and we will have him ready for your punk ass. Now get the fuck out of my building.

Fist looked from Kenyatta to Young as he snatched the paper from his hand. He looked at the address and gave a sly grin.

"Y'all niggas don't have a clue, but y'all will not fuck my son up with y'all bullshit. I'll see yo' ass in an hour." With that he turned and walked out the office.

Kenyatta was staring at the space vacated by Lil' Young. For the life of him he couldn't figure out why the three of them couldn't get it right. Young walked over to the desk and leaned on it.

"No need in looking like that. He doesn't want to be here and I refuse to kiss his ass, so give him his son and let's get this money. I don't want to hear shit else about it. It's taking everything in me not to pop his arrogant ass."

As Young turned to leave, Kenyatta's phone rang. He answered the phone and listened as the person on the other end talked. He screamed out, "What the fuck! Okay, don't go home!" When he hung up the phone Young was looking at him curiously. Kenyatta pushed a button on his desk and the wall to the left of him opened up. He moved quickly and entered his gun safe. He grabbed his AK, and twin glocks. Snatching up extra ammo, he looked at his Pop's and said,

"He is fucking DEAD!"

Take Down

The sun was working overtime today. He was glad he had gotten the darkest tint allowed in his state, on his windows. It not only keeps the sun out, but drivers from looking in. There wasn't a cloud in the sky as Fist sat in his burgundy Suburban with KEM playing low in the background. There was something about KEM's sound he found soothing. Right now that's exactly what he needed, something soothing. It was taking everything in him not to turn his truck around and head back to TNT and shoot the whole building up. Every time the thought came to his mind, he would picture the nice old lady and her welcoming smile, and sit back and allow KEM to take over. He closed his eyes and let the groove penetrate his psyche. Fist realized he has really been on edge for over ten years. It was now time to let shit go. He was going to wash his brain of Kenyatta, Young and everything that smelled like them. He was about to be a father. There was going to be a person who looked up to him like he used to look up to his father, only he would never let him down.

Fist opened his eyes as his senses began to tingle. He learned to pay attention to this feeling; it served him well over the years. There were two entrances to the street. Both seemed to be flooded with cars in an affluent neighborhood in the middle of the day. Something about that shit wasn't setting right with him. He popped the floor board on the passenger side, retrieved his heat and got ready to move.

Wanda Lee saw the Suburban Kenyatta said that Lil' Young was driving in front of the house. She couldn't see inside because of the dark tint. Even after a year, she was feeling like she had a score to settle with him for choking her out. She was willing to push it aside on the strength of Young, but now it looks like she has been given the green light. Wanda Lee didn't question her good fortune, she just mounted up for the ride. Her instructions were to pin him down until Kenyatta and Young made it to the scene. But she was really hoping Lil' Young wanted to play, so she could do her thing. Blocking the truck in with a car in the back, the front and on the driver side, she was trying to make a big statement.

Fist looked out his driver side window and rear view mirror. The shit would be comical if it wasn't so real. He couldn't believe these motherfuckers came for him. Shaking his head, he checked his ankle holster and extra ammo. He smiled cryptically because they had no clue who the fuck he was. Moving in stealth mode, he made his way to the back seat on his stomach. He screwed the evolution silencer into the glock and aimed through the custom hole in the trunk.

"Psst, psst." That's what it sounded like leaving his glock. The car blocking him in the rear now had twin holes in the driver window. Fist quickly opened the passenger rear door and crawled out. He knelt down and duck walked to the front of the truck and aimed at the car that was blocking him in the front. "Psst, psst." *Two more down; these clowns are slipping.* Tires screeching and multiple doors slamming could be heard. Fist said to himself, *Game Time!*

Fist Full Of Tears: The Sequel

Kenyatta and Young met Wanda Lee and Juice in the middle of the street. Everyone was packing enough heat to create a war zone.

> "He hasn't said a word," Wanda Lee said as she looked towards the truck.

Kenyatta wasn't trying to have any small talk. He wanted the bitch that shot his mother. He aimed his gun and started shooting, moving on pure hatred.

> "Lil' Young, where is Joselyn? Send the bitch out," Young shouted over his son's gun fire.

Young told Wanda Lee to have the other Young Gunz move in on the truck. He held his hand up to Kenyatta for him to stop shooting. Wanda Lee could be heard calling out to Dizzy and B who were in the car that blocked the truck from the front, but she didn't get an answer. Juice walked over to the car and what he saw made him turn and aim his weapon towards the truck. "Psst, psst;" he was to slow. Juice's body crumpled to the ground in a heap. Everyone moved at once as they opened fire on the truck.

****

Lynette was at her parent's house with baby Young and Lania. Her calls to Kenyatta continued to go straight to voicemail and that was gyrating on her nerves. She was walking back and forth in the den with her cell phone in her hand and her finger on the redial button.

"Lynette sit down somewhere, you are about to give me palpitations," her mother said while holding her hand over her heart.

Giving her mother a side-eye look, she walked over to the bay window and hit redial again. Once again the phone went straight to voice mail and that was the last straw. Lynette went about gathering the baby by placing him back in his car seat.
When she went to get Lania, her mother stood in her path with her arms folded across her chest.

"I don't know what you are mixed up in now, but this child is staying here. Now although I want that sweet baby to stay here as well, I'm not going to get in the middle of that. But this child here, my beautiful grandbaby, will be here when you get back." With that she picked Lania up and moved towards the back of the house.

Lynette didn't have the energy to argue with her mother. Perhaps leaving Lania here until she dealt with this situation was for the best. Without even saying so much as goodbye, Lynette grabbed baby Young's car seat and baby bag, and headed out the door. She was determined to find out what the hell was going on.

****

The Courthouse Estates was definitely a war zone. Kenyatta, Young and Wanda Lee moved in a swarm in order to surround the truck. The fire power coming from each of them would continue simultaneously with their movements. The Suburban was taking some heavy hits, but it wasn't fazed.

Fist Full Of Tears: The Sequel

It was a custom bullet proof truck and was up for whatever challenge they could bring. No one noticed the yellow cab pulling up on the other side of Kenyatta's truck. Joselyn paid the driver after telling him to back out of the street as quietly as possible. The driver was from the hood so he knew how to stick and move. Digging in her Marc Jacobs backpack, she was silently thankful she kept her heat and clips with her. Joselyn didn't hesitate to pull out.

There was no way she was going to let them pin her man down without putting some bullets in their ass. She jumped out of the cab spitting fire from her custom made Mac-10, determined to help Fist. Her first shot entered Wanda Lee's shoulder and spun her around like the scarecrow from "The Wiz", but like a beast, Wanda Lee swung her arm and fired in Joselyn's direction saying,

> "Welcome to the party we are throwing in your honor." Wanda's laughter could be heard over all the gunfire.

Kenyatta spotted Joselyn in a heated battle with Wanda Lee. They were going hard, but Wanda Lee was coming up short. He felt like he was having an out of body experience as he watched Wanda Lee take a shot to the face. Her piercing scream was enough to push him into action. Aiming his gun at the woman responsible for taking the light out of his mother's eyes, it also hit him she was the reason baby Louis would never know the full value of the love his mother carried. Kenyatta's anger was boiling over and he went full speed running towards Joselyn busting both of his guns.

"Die hard you useless bitch," Kenyatta said as three of his bullets found a home in Joselyn's chest.

There was no description for the peace that fell over him as he watched Joselyn's body crumple to the ground.

"Nooooooooooooooooooooo,"

Fist screamed deep in his soul as he saw the love of his life lying on the hot concrete. Once again he was the cause of her being somewhere she shouldn't be, but this time she paid the ultimate price.
Busting at Kenyatta and Young at the same damn time, Fist was trying to right the wrongs in his life. He wanted to end them both and in doing so, find some type of peace.

"You are out gunned and out matched. I don't want to dishonor the memory of your mother by killing you, but on everything, if you don't get in your truck and leave now I'm gonna send you to hell." Young was every bit the killer that his legend said he was.

The problem with most people is they think they are more than they are. Fist knew this to be true of his father. He used to think the man was bigger than life. Not having him in his life left a huge hole in his heart. Over the last year Fist had to let a lot of shit go; and one of those things was his desire to have a real fucking family.

"Fuck you old man!"

Fist Full Of Tears: The Sequel

Fist shot Kenyatta in the head killing him instantly. He turned both of his weapons on Young with a sly smile on his face.

> "It's just you and me, just like old times; except this time, I hate your fucking guts."

The gunfire sounded like thunder clouds or a massive explosion. The reality was it was the sound of the end of an era. A powerful mixture of hatred and love pushed Fist to pull the trigger on the man who gave him life. He couldn't control what his heart was telling him must be done. The shots hit their mark and Young was hit in the chest and eye. He fell to one knee and death was imminent.

Fist never got a chance to enjoy the site of his father falling to his knees because Young got two shots off before he went down. If nothing else, Young was an excellent shot even as he was dying. Fist was hit in the neck and gut. He fell forward and was bleeding profusely from his neck wound. A lot of scenes passed through his mind as he felt his life slipping away, but the thing he would most regret was not being able to hold his child.

When Lynette pulled up to her home, tears immediately started sliding down her face. She could see Kenyatta lying on the ground with all of the life gone from his body. She didn't think she could ever feel this level of hurt. Surveying the street, she could tell everyone was dead; Young, Kenyatta and Lil' Young. *They killed each other* she said to herself as she heard sirens in the distance. She was both horrified and sick to her stomach. She made her way quickly back to her car to a peaceful and sleeping baby Young.

He was so pure and unaffected by all of the hate and death that consumed his family. In an instant Lynette made a decision. Looking back at baby Young she said,

> "You are the future and I promise you I will never let anything happen to you."

Lynette started the car and slowly drove down the street determined Louis Young, III would never carry a *fist full of tears*.

The End

I hope you enjoyed Fist Full of Tears. As always I appreciate you taking your time out and reading my work…… Turn the page to read a synopsis of my upcoming work.

Moon

Fanita Moon Pendleton

Catch up on all the Criminal Romance you can handle from Fanita Moon Pendleton Available in Kindle and Paperback! www.urbanmoonbooksandmore.com

Fist Full Of Tears: The Sequel

Now Available from Fanita Moon Pendleton

Open Marriage: A Fatal Attraction Love Story

The Grass is not Always Greener

Lust and Love are in a tug a war in this tale of a marriage stretched to its limit.

Bri wears sexy like it's a next skin. She is every man's dream wife; successful and sinful. But does she want too much?

Jason is the envy of all his boys and on the wish list of every woman with a pulse. But after marrying Bri another woman didn't stand a chance.

Lies and Deceit threaten to cause cracks in this marriage as everyone wants in and no one wants out. Enter a world where love and happiness is a risk worth taking.

Fanita Moon Pendleton

Coming Soon From Fanita Moon Pendleton!

Moet's Revenge

What Happens in Vegas……

Moet didn't set out to be a Boss. She actually had a different plan for her life, but sometimes tragedy will make you who you really are.

Harry Blake was born into the life. The streets called him Killa, and he was damn good at it. The only soft spot in his heart belonged to one woman, finding what to do with those feelings is a different story.

Follow Moet as she discovers the inner strength to deal with her deep scars and emotions. Through it all she will learn how to Act Like A *Lady* and Think Like A *Boss.*

About The Author

Born and raised in Oakland California, Fanita Pendleton relocated to Norfolk Virginia during her senior year in high school, and has called the magnificent city home ever since. Fanita began her career as a Juvenile Probation Officer and later worked in Adult Probation before taking a short break to pursue her love of teaching as a Criminal Justice Instructor at a local technical college. Recently Fanita stepped back into law enforcement, and is now a Parole Officer.

Fanita blazed on the scene with her Criminal Romance Series: Shoot First Ask Questions Never, Fist Full of Tears, The Moscato Diaries, Act Like A Lady, Think Like A Boss: Vegas…MOET: Money Over Everything. An avid reader, Fanita holds a special place in her heart for the unsung genre of Urban Crime and Urban Romance Dramas, and in her youth, devoured the works of such greats as Donald Goines, and Iceberg Slim. Fanita is Owner Urban Moon Books where she is now giving young authors their shot at making their dreams come true.

Fanita received her Master's Degree in Public Administration from Troy University, as well as a Bachelors in Sociology from Langston University, and her Associates in Communications from Luzerne County Community College. She enjoys shooting pool, both for league and leisure, and catching a football, or basketball game with her son, the inspiration of her dreams. Connect with Fanita on Facebook "Fanita Moon Pendleton", Instagram #FanitaPendleton, Twitter @Moon081471 or through her website http://www.urbanmoonproductions.com

Fanita Moon Pendleton